BAUMGARTNER

Also by Paul Auster

PAUL AUSTER

BAUMGARTNER

a novel

Grove Press

New York

FIRST EDITION

Published simultaneously in Canada
Printed in the United States of America

The interior of this book was designed by Norman E. Tuttle
at Alpha Design & Composition.
This book was set in 11.5-pt. Adobe Caslon
by Alpha Design & Composition of Pittsfield, NH.

First Grove Atlantic hardcover edition: November 2023

Library of Congress Cataloging-in-Publication data
is available for this title.

ISBN 978-0-8021-6144-4
eISBN 978-0-8021-6153-6

Grove Press
an imprint of Grove Atlantic
154 West 14th Street
New York, NY 10011

Distributed by Publishers Group West

groveatlantic.com

23 24 25 26   10 9 8 7 6 5 4 3 2 1

BAUMGARTNER

1

Baumgartner is sitting at his desk in the second-floor room he variously refers to as his study, his cogitorium, and his hole. Pen in hand, he is midway through a sentence in the third chapter of his monograph on Kierkegaard's pseudonyms when it occurs to him that the book he needs to quote from in order to finish the sentence is downstairs in the living room, where he left it before going up to bed last night. On the way downstairs to retrieve the book, it also occurs to him that he promised to call his sister this morning at ten o'clock, and since it is almost ten now, he decides that he will go into the kitchen and make the call before retrieving the book from the living room. When he walks into the kitchen, however, he is stopped in his tracks by a sharp, stinging smell. Something is burning, he realizes, and as he advances toward the stove, he sees that one of the front burners has been left on and that a low, persistent flame is eating its way into the bottom of the small aluminum pot he used three hours ago to cook his breakfast of two soft-boiled eggs. He turns off the burner, and then, without thinking twice, that is, without bothering to fetch a pot holder or a towel, he lifts the destroyed, smoldering egg boiler off the stove and scalds his hand. Baumgartner cries out in pain. A fraction of a second later, he drops the pot, which hits the floor with an abrupt, clattering ping, and then, still yelping in pain, he rushes over to the sink, turns on the cold water, sticks his right hand under the spout, and holds it there for the next three or four minutes as the chilly stream pours down over his skin.

Hoping he has warded off any potential blisters on his fingers and palm, Baumgartner cautiously dries off his hand with a dish towel, pauses for a moment to flex his fingers, pats his hand with the towel a couple of more times, and then asks himself what he is doing in the kitchen. Before he can remember that he is supposed to be calling his sister, the telephone rings. He lifts the receiver off the hook and mumbles forth a guarded hello. His sister, he says to himself, finally remembering why he is here, and now that it is past ten and he has failed to call her, he fully expects Naomi to be the person on the other end of the line, his cantankerous younger sister who will no doubt begin the conversation by scolding him for having forgotten to call her *again, as he always does*, but once the person on the other end begins to speak, it turns out not to be Naomi but a man, an unknown man with an unfamiliar voice who is stammering out some sort of apology to him for being late. Late for what? Baumgartner asks. To read your meter, the man says. I was supposed to be there at nine, remember? No, Baumgartner doesn't remember, he can't recall a single moment in the past days or weeks when he thought the meter reader from the electric company was scheduled to be there at nine, and therefore he tells the man not to worry about it, he plans to be home all morning and afternoon, but the electric company man, who sounds young and inexperienced and eager to please, insists on explaining that he has no time to explain just now why he didn't show up on time, but there was *a good reason* for it, a reason *beyond his control*, and that he will be there as soon as he can. Fine, Baumgartner says, I'll see you then. He hangs up and looks down at his right hand, which has begun to throb from the burn, but when he examines his palm and fingers, he sees no signs of blistering or peeling skin, just a general sort of redness. Not so bad, he thinks, I can live with that, and then, addressing himself in the second person, he thinks, You stupid ass, consider yourself lucky.

It occurs to him that he should call Naomi now, on the spot, *to head her off at the pass*, but just as he lifts the receiver off the hook to dial her number, the doorbell rings. A prolonged sigh emerges from Baumgartner's lungs. With the dial tone still buzzing in his hand, he hangs up the receiver and begins walking toward the front of the house, grumpily kicking aside the scorched pot as he heads out of the kitchen.

His mood brightens when he opens the door and sees that it is the UPS woman, Molly, a frequent visitor who over time has acquired the status of . . . of what? Not quite a friend, exactly, but more than just an acquaintance by now, given that she has been coming to the door two or three times a week for the past five years, and the truth is that the lonely Baumgartner, whose wife has been dead for close to a decade, has a secret crush on this chunky woman in her mid-thirties whose last name he doesn't even know, for even if Molly is black and his wife was not, there is something in her eyes that makes him think of his dead Anna whenever he looks at her. It never fails to happen, but precisely what that thing is he is hard-pressed to say. A sense of alertness, perhaps, although it is a good deal more than that, or else something that could be described as a *radiant vigilance*, or else, if not that, quite simply the power of an *illuminated self-hood*, human aliveness in all its vibratory splendor emanating from within to without in a complex, interlocking dance of feeling and thought—something like that, perhaps, if such a thing makes any sense, but whatever you want to call the thing that Anna had, Molly has it as well. For that reason, Baumgartner has taken to ordering books he does not need and will never open and will end up donating to the local public library for the sole purpose of spending a minute or two in Molly's company every time she rings the bell to deliver one of the books.

Good morning, Professor, she says, smiling her illuminated smile at him as if it were a benediction. Another book for you.

Thank you, Molly, Baumgartner says, smiling back at her as she hands him the slender brown package. How are you doing today?

It's early yet—too soon to tell—but so far the ups are more up than the downs are down. It's hard to feel blue on a gorgeous morning like this one.

The first good day of spring—the best day of the year. Let's enjoy it while we can, Molly. You never know what's going to happen next.

Ain't that the truth, Molly replies. She lets out a short, complicitous laugh, and then, before he can think of some clever or amusing response that would prolong the conversation, she is waving good-bye to him and walking back to her truck.

That is another one of the many things Baumgartner likes about Molly. She always laughs at his lame remarks, even the most feeble ones, the out-and-out duds.

He walks back into the kitchen and deposits the unopened book package on top of the pile of other unopened book packages wedged into a corner of the room near the table. The tower has grown so high of late that it looks as if one or two more of those pale brown rectangles will topple the whole thing over. Baumgartner makes a mental note to remove the books from their cardboard enclosures at some point later in the day and transfer the naked books to the least full of the several cartons sitting on the back porch that have been set aside with other unwanted books for donation to the public library. Yes, yes, Baumgartner says to himself, I know I promised to do that the last time Molly was here, and the time before that as well, but this time I really mean it.

He looks at his watch and sees that it is ten-fifteen. Getting late, he thinks, but perhaps not too late to call Naomi and head her off at the pass before she can begin showering him with foulmouthed insults. He reaches for the phone, but just as he is about to lift it off the hook, the little white devil rings again. Again, he assumes it is his sister, and again he is wrong.

A small, trembling voice answers his mumbled hello with a barely audible question: *Mr. Baumgartner?* The words are spoken by someone so young and so clearly in distress that Baumgartner is flooded with alarm, as if every organ in his body were suddenly working at twice its normal speed. When he asks who it is, the voice says *Rosita*, and all at once he knows that something must have happened to Mrs. Flores, the woman who first came to clean the house a few days after Anna's funeral and has been coming twice a week since then to mop the floors and vacuum the rugs and tend to his laundry and handle numerous other household chores that have prevented him from living in squalor and disarray for the past nine and a half years, the good and steady and mostly silent, walled-off Mrs. Flores, with her construction-worker husband and three children, the two grown boys and the youngest one, Rosita, a skinny twelve-year-old with magnificent brown eyes who comes to the house every year on Halloween for her little bag of goodies.

What's wrong, Rosita? Baumgartner asks. Has something happened to your mother?

No, Rosita says, not my mother. My father.

Baumgartner waits for several moments as the girl's pent-up tears spill out of her in a short, stifled crying fit, and because the little one is struggling to hold herself together and will not allow herself to let go completely, her breath has turned into a series of chopped-off gasps and shudderings. Baumgartner understands that because Mrs. Flores was scheduled to come to the house this afternoon, and because it is spring break and her daughter is not at school, she has instructed Rosita to call Mr. Baumgartner about the emergency while she herself goes off to confront whatever it is that has happened to her husband.

Once the gasps and choked-off tears have subsided somewhat, Baumgartner asks the next question. By piecing together the girl's fragmented account of what her mother told her, who herself had heard it from someone else, he gathers that Mr. Flores was on a kitchen remodeling job this morning, and as he was down in the client's basement cutting two-by-fours with his buzz saw, an operation he has performed hundreds if not thousands of times in the past, he somehow managed to slice off two of the fingers on his right hand.

Baumgartner sees the two severed fingers falling into a pile of sawdust on the floor. He sees the blood flowing from the bare, skinless stumps. He hears Mr. Flores scream.

At last he says: Don't worry, Rosita. I know it sounds terrible, but the doctors can fix it. They can reattach your father's fingers to the hand, and by the time you start school again in the fall, he'll be in perfect shape.

Really?

Yes, really. I promise.

Because the girl is alone in the house, and because she has been locked in a state of pure, petrified panic ever since her mother left for the hospital, Baumgartner goes on talking to her for another ten minutes. At one point toward the end of the conversation, he manages to coax something that resembles a laugh from her, and when they finally hang up, that tiny excuse of a laugh is what stays with him, for he is almost certain it will stand as the single most important thing he has accomplished all day.

Nevertheless, Baumgartner is shaken. He pulls out a chair and sits down, fixing his eyes on the black ring of an old coffee-cup stain as he walks through the scene in his mind. Angel Flores, a veteran carpenter of forty-eight, in the act of doing something he has done repeatedly and successfully over the course of many years, suddenly and unaccountably slips up and, through a single moment's inattention, gravely injures himself. Why? What caused him to lose his concentration and turn his thoughts from the task at hand, which is a simple one if you are concentrating and a dangerous one if you are not? Had one of his co-workers distracted him by walking down the stairs at that moment? Had a stray thought inadvertently entered his head? Had a fly landed on his nose? Had he felt a sudden pain in his stomach? Had he drunk too much last night or quarreled with his wife before leaving the house or . . . It suddenly occurs to him that perhaps Mr. Flores was cutting off his fingers at the precise moment that he, Baumgartner, was burning his hand on the pot. Each one the cause of his own misery, even if one's misery was far greater than the other's, and yet, in each case—

The doorbell rings, interrupting the flow of Baumgartner's wandering thoughts. Damn it, he says, as he slowly rises from the chair and shuffles toward the front of the house, They won't even let a man think around here.

When Baumgartner opens the front door, he finds himself looking into the face of the meter reader, a tall, strapping fellow in his late twenties or early thirties dressed in the electric company's regulation blue shirt, with a PSE&G logo emblazoned on the left pocket and, just under it, in vivid yellow stitching, the name of the man inside the shirt: Ed. As far as Baumgartner can tell, the look in Ed's eyes is both hopeful and distraught. A strange combination, he thinks, and when Ed offers a tentative smile by way of greeting, the effect is even more confusing—as if the meter reader is half expecting the door to be slammed in his face. To allay the man's anxieties, Baumgartner invites him into the house.

Thank you, Mr. Boom Garden, the man says, as he strides across the threshold. I appreciate it.

More amused than miffed by the mangling of his name, Baumgartner says: Why don't we call each other by our first names? I already know yours—Ed—so why don't you drop the mister stuff and call me Sy?

Sigh? says Ed. What kind of a name is that?

Not the sigh you make with your breath—just Sy, S-Y. It's short for Seymour, the ridiculous name my parents gave me when I was born. Sy is no great shakes, I admit, but at least it's better than Seymour.

You, too, huh? says the meter reader.

Me, too, what? says Baumgartner.

Stuck with a name you don't like.

What's wrong with Ed?

Nothing. It's the last name that bugs me.

Oh? And what is it?

Papadopoulos.

Nothing wrong with that. It's a fine Greek name.

For someone who lives in Greece, maybe. But it makes people in America laugh. The other kids laughed at me when I was in school, and when I was pitching A-ball a few years back, the whole crowd would laugh when they heard my name announced over the loudspeaker. It gives a guy a what-do-you-call-it. A complex.

If it bothers you so much, why don't you change it?

I can't. It would break my father's heart.

Baumgartner is growing bored. If he doesn't put a halt to these meandering irrelevancies, Ed Papadopoulos will soon be spouting his father's entire life story to him or reminiscing about his up-and-down career in the low minor leagues, so Sy, short for Seymour, abruptly changes the topic and asks Ed if he would like to take a look at the meter in the basement. That is when he learns that this is the young man's first day on the job and that the meter downstairs will be the first one he has ever read as a full-fledged employee of the Public Service Electric & Gas Company, which explains why he did not show up at the appointed time—not through any fault of his own, mind you, but because a gang of veteran meter readers on the staff played a joke on him this morning—his first morning on the job!—and emptied the gas tank in his van, leaving him with enough fuel to travel only half a mile, which caused the van to stall out on a crowded road in heavy rush hour traffic and led to the embarrassing delay. He is sorry, he says, so terribly sorry for inconveniencing him. If only he'd had the good sense to check the gas gauge before going off on his rounds, he would have been here on time, but those stupid pranksters had to play their joke on him, just because he's the new kid on the block, and watch and see if he doesn't catch hell from the supervisor for it. Another one of these screwups, and he'll be put on probation. Two more, and he'll probably be canned.

By now, Baumgartner is ready to scream. From whence came this brawny motormouth, he asks himself, and by what means can this inexhaustible flow of words be stopped? And yet, in spite of his growing irritation, he can't help feeling some sympathy for this good-natured oaf, so rather than open his lungs and let forth with a full-throated howl, Baumgartner emits a soft, almost inaudible sigh and begins walking toward the door that leads to the basement.

It's down there, he says, on the back wall to the left, but when he flicks the switch to turn on the basement light, the basement remains dark. Damn it, Baumgartner says, struggling not to lose control of himself, in the same way little Rosita had struggled not to cry when they talked earlier, The bulb down there must have burned out.

No problem, says Ed. I have a flashlight. Standard equipment, you know.

Good. I'm sure you'll be able to find it.

Maybe yes, maybe no, says the novice meter reader. You wouldn't mind going down to show me where it is, would you? Just this once, so I won't waste any more of your time.

It occurs to Baumgartner that Ed Papadopoulos is afraid of the dark, or perhaps just afraid of dark basements, especially in old houses like this one, with spiderwebs dangling from the beams and giant bugs scampering along the floor and God knows what invisible objects blocking passage to the meter, and therefore, even though he has no doubt that Naomi will call him the instant his foot touches the bottom step, Baumgartner reluctantly allows himself to be talked into leading the way.

The stairs to the basement are wobbly and decrepit, one more thing that Baumgartner has promised himself to repair and still hasn't, not even after years of making the same promise with the same sense of earnest resolve, for it never occurs to him to think about the stairs until he finds himself walking down to the basement, and once he goes up again and shuts the door, he forgets all about them. Now, with no overhead light to illuminate the stairs, and with the only source of light coming from Ed's flashlight behind him, Baumgartner warily takes hold of the splintered wooden railing, but no sooner does he tighten his grip around it than his scorched palm and fingers are jabbed by a thousand phantom needles—as if he were being burned again. He instantly draws back the hand, and because there is no railing on the left, he has nothing to hold on to anymore, but still, confident that he knows these stairs well after living in this house for so many years, he hazards a first step downward, misses the plank by half an inch, loses his balance in the dark, and tumbles down to the bottom, bashing an elbow, bashing the other elbow, and then cracking his right knee against the hard cement floor.

For the second time that morning, Baumgartner cries out in pain.

The cry dissipates into a prolonged spasm of groans as his crumpled-up body twists around on the dank floor.

He has no idea that his limbs are moving, but he nevertheless knows that he is still conscious, for a number of
disconnected thoughts are bouncing around in his head,
even if those thoughts are dim and incomprehensible to
him, which would disqualify them as true thoughts, he
supposes, and relegate them to the category of almost-
thoughts or non-thoughts, except perhaps that in spite of
the pain assaulting his elbows and right knee, there is no
pain in his head, which would suggest that his skull has
survived the fall without any serious knocks, which in turn
would suggest that when all is said and done the accident
will not have turned him into a blithering, drooling idiot
ripe for the glue factory. A moment later, however, when
Ed is standing over him and shining the flashlight in his
face, Baumgartner is unable to summon the words to tell
him to turn the light elsewhere and instead lets out another
groan as he puts his right hand over his eyes. This inabil-
ity to articulate his thoughts troubles him, even frightens
him. If nothing else, it proves that the brainworks are still
scrambled, if not permanently damaged after all, or else
merely gummed up for the time being by the pain that has
gone on digging into various body parts other than his head,
his right elbow in particular, which felt as if it would burst
into flames when he lifted his arm to cover his eyes with
his hand, the same right hand that has already been burned
this morning and is still aching now, no doubt because he
broke the final stage of his fall by thrusting out his hands

as he hit the cement floor at the bottom, even though he has no memory of doing that.

Holy shit, Ed says. Are you all right?

After a long pause, Baumgartner at last manages to push some words out of his mouth. Hard to say, he says. Gratifying as it is to learn that he has not lost the power of speech, the pain is still too strong for him to exult in the victory. At least I'm not dead, he continues. There's something to be said for that, I suppose.

Of course there is, replies the meter man, there's everything to be said for it. But tell me, Sy, where does it hurt?

As Baumgartner enumerates the banged-up places on his body, Ed, slipping into the role of professional sports trainer, carefully assesses the potential damage to each battered muscle, tendon, and bone, and once the inventory is complete, he asks Baumgartner if he has the strength to be lifted off the ground and guided up the stairs.

Let's give it a shot, Baumgartner says. If I can't make it, we'll know soon enough.

So Ed Papadopoulos, a stranger who entered Baumgartner's house no more than ten minutes ago, hoists the old man from the ground with his right hand as he holds the flashlight with his left, and then, with his right arm firmly clamped around Baumgartner's ribs and torso, begins the laborious process of maneuvering him up the narrow, rickety stairs. Of all the things that hurt, Baumgartner discovers, it is the knee that hurts the most, hurts so much that merely to stand on it produces a yowling sort of pain, such yowls as to mimic the discord and clamor of forty screeching bobcats, and yet, spurred on by his gratitude for Ed's solicitous care and capable, muscular arm, Baumgartner is determined to do his best and not complain, to bear up to the yowls and shrieks in steadfast, stoical silence. Therefore, even when Ed launches into an account of his own knee injury four years ago, a torn meniscus that put him on the shelf for most of the season and ultimately destroyed his pitching career, Baumgartner emits no sound but for an occasional grunt, nor does he speak or cry out when Ed goes on to explain that once he returned from his injury his heater had lost its sting and his curve had lost its snap, and there it was, he says, So long Charlie, it's been nice to know ya, and even then, as Baumgartner remains trapped within the ex-pitcher's long-winded tale of broken dreams and cups of coffee that were never drunk, which lasts throughout the entire four minutes it takes to ascend the stairs, he does not hold it against Ed and in fact clings to the meter reader's words as a grim but welcome distraction from the pain.

Once they make it to the top of the stairs, Baumgartner continues to lean on Ed as he hobbles forward into the living room, where his protector eases him onto the sofa and then props up his head with a pair of embroidered pillows. We should put some ice on that knee, the young man says, and before Baumgartner can tell him that the ice machine in the refrigerator is broken, Ed disappears from the room.

Baumgartner listens as the freezer compartment is opened and then closed. A few seconds later, Ed reappears, looking both befuddled and chagrined. No ice, he says, speaking in the same forlorn tone as a child who has just discovered there is no Santa Claus or an adolescent searcher who has just discovered there is no God or a dying man who has just discovered there is no tomorrow.

Don't worry about it, Baumgartner says, I'll be fine.

I don't know about that, the meter man says. You look pretty banged up, Sy. Hair all disheveled, your pants all smudgy and stained. We should probably get you to the hospital for some X-rays. Just to make sure nothing's broken.

Forget it, Baumgartner says. No hospital, no X-rays. All I need is a little rest, a chance to regroup. I'll be up and about in no time.

Well, suit yourself, Ed says, looking over his patient carefully as small, invisible wheels begin to turn in his head. At least let me get you a glass of water, okay?

Thank you. A glass of water would be lovely.

A minute and a half later, as Baumgartner is drinking the water, Ed abruptly sits down on the floor and leans forward until his face is almost touching Baumgartner's. Tell me, Sy, he asks, what year is it?

Baumgartner pauses in mid-sip, gulps down the water gathered in his mouth, and says: What kind of a question is that?

Just humor me, Sy. What year is it?

Well, let's see. If we can eliminate 1906 and 1687, along with 1777 and 1944, then it must be 2018. How's that? Close enough?

Ed smiles and says: Right down the middle of the plate. Satisfied?

Two or three more—just for the fun of it.

Sighing deeply with exasperation, Baumgartner ponders whether to pop Ed in the snout or to play along out of politeness. He shuts his eyes, poised at the crossroads between crotchety old grump and otherworldly sage, and finally says, All right, doctor. Next question.

Where are we?

Where? Why, we're here, of course, where we always are—each one of us locked in his or her here from the moment we're born until the day we die.

True enough, but I'm thinking more along the lines of what town we're in. The place on the map that the two of us are in right now.

Well, in that case, we're in Princeton, aren't we? Princeton, New Jersey, to be exact. A beautiful but dreary place in my opinion, but that's only my opinion. What do you think?

I don't know. I've never been here before. It looks pretty nice to me, but I don't live here the way you do, so I can't really say.

Baumgartner wants to go on teasing Ed as they march through the remaining questions, but he can't bring himself to do it. The force of the young man's goodwill overwhelms any impulse to mock him, and so once the little Q&A is finished and the meter man is satisfied that his patient has no concussion or other life-threatening symptoms, Baumgartner tells him that he has already taken up enough of his time and that he should be off on his rounds again, lickety-split, since there are more meters to be read today, which suddenly reminds Ed that in all the confusion following Baumgartner's tumble down the stairs, he has forgotten to read the meter, and just like that he grabs hold of his flashlight and hustles out of the room to complete his first job as an official member of the PSE&G staff.

As Baumgartner listens to the sound of boots clomping down the basement stairs, he reflects on the curious skein of circumstances that have put him on his back with a pair of throbbing elbows and a swollen, aching knee, which no doubt will cause him to walk with a limp for the next several weeks, if not to the end of the summer or perhaps even to the end of his life. Nothing to be done about that, he says to himself, and then his thoughts turn to poor Mr. Flores and that dreadful business of the two chopped-off fingers. How horrible it must have been to see himself doing that to his own body, Baumgartner thinks, not just watching his fingers fall off his hand but knowing that he himself was responsible for his own mutilation. From all he has heard, doctors can routinely sew back severed fingers these days and get them working normally again, but he doesn't know anyone who has personally experienced one of those miraculous restorations and therefore hopes he was not lying to Rosita when he promised that her father would eventually be whole again, for one must never lie to children, *never*, not under any circumstances, even if that rule can sometimes be broken when it comes to adults.

By now he has forgotten all about his Kierkegaard essay and the book he was planning to carry upstairs in order to polish off the sentence he was writing. He has also forgotten about the phone call to his sister and the fact that he ever had a sister to begin with, for so much has happened since those things were important, pressing matters to him that they might as well have been part of someone else's life. For the time being, his only plans are to go on resting for a while and wait for Ed to return from his meter work below, at which point he will thank him for his many kindnesses and send him on his way. He closes his eyes, and for the next minute or two his thoughts continue to drift from this thing to that thing, but before long there are no things and the thoughts have been replaced by a succession of dream images, most of them of Anna when Anna was young, and one by one he sees her smiling at him and frowning at him and spinning across a room somewhere and sitting in a chair somewhere and standing on her toes and stretching her arms toward the ceiling.

When he wakes up, the light trickling into the room suggests that some time has passed. Baumgartner assumes it has been no more than twelve or fifteen minutes, but when he looks at his watch, the dial says ten to one, which means that he has been out cold for forty-five minutes or an hour. He glances over at the coffee table immediately to his right and sees that a handwritten note is lying on top of a pile of books. If he wants to read it, he will have to extend his right arm in order to snag the sheet with his fingertips, which will further call upon him to test the condition of his elbow, but what the hell, he thinks, be a brave boy and do it, and so Baumgartner does it, and while the elbow is sore and painful, the pain is not so terrible as to require anything more than a loud grunt.

Dear Sy, You were asleep when I got upstairs. I didn't want to disturb you so I left. When I'm done working I'll go to the store and get you a bag of ice. It will help your knee and cut down the swelling. I'll also get a new lightbulb for your basement. Expect me between 6 and 6:30. Sincerely yours, Ed Papadopoulos.

Extraordinary, Baumgartner says to himself. A perfect stranger going out of his way to do all that. In a world full of shitheads and selfish brutes, along comes this good-hearted innocent as an angel of mercy, and yes, the ice will surely help, since the knee is exceedingly tender and the flesh around the patella is bloated now, spongy with blood and damaged tissue or whatever it is that gathers under the skin when a part of the body begins to swell.

Baumgartner makes a mental note to call Ed's supervisor at PSE&G and gush enthusiastically about the outstanding qualities of the new man on his team.

21

The only telephone on the ground floor is in the kitchen, and when Baumgartner thinks about going to the kitchen, he understands that he is hungry, so hungry that he decides that when and if he can manage to walk that far, he will not only make the call to PSE&G but rustle up some lunch for himself as well.

Rolling off the sofa is less difficult than he imagined it would be, but standing up proves to be a torture, as does the act of moving his right leg forward, especially when he plants his right foot on the floor. Grunting helps a bit, but not much, and while hopping across the room on his left leg would be the ideal solution, he is afraid he would lose his balance and fall, even though he was once considered a fine athlete, one of the best in his school when he was young, but that was a long time ago now, a whole lifetime ago when you stop and think about how many years have gone by since then, and Baumgartner understands how foolish it would be even to consider taking that risk, in spite of the fact that he was once capable of taking hold of his left foot with his right hand and jumping over his left leg with his right leg without letting go of the left foot with the right hand. It was a feat that inspired awe among his friends and made the girls gasp, for he was the only person who could pull off that bizarre, mindless stunt, but that was then and this is now, he says to himself, and for now he has no choice but to hobble and grunt his way to the kitchen with slow, cautious steps and pray he doesn't collapse before he gets there.

He nearly collapses but doesn't, he nearly doesn't make it
but does, and once he crosses the finish line he is so drained by
his exertions that he plops himself down in one of the chairs
spread around the kitchen table. Needless to say, it is the one
closest to the door he has just walked through, but it is also
the only one from which a person can look out the window
and see the entire backyard and, by turning his head slightly in
another direction, see the entire room as well. Breathing hard
and hammered by what he has just been through, Baumgartner
knows it will be a long while before he can stand up again and
make the journey from the chair to the cupboard and then
to the fridge and the stove and the sink and the wall phone,
and for now he just sits there in a fog of pain and exhaus-
tion, indifferent as to where he is looking or what he is seeing or even if he is seeing anything at all. As it happens, he
has landed in the chair in such a way that his head is turned
in the direction of the room, and as his breathing gradually
subsides to a more or less normal rhythm, he begins to cast
his eyes around the room and eventually catches sight of the
scorched pot on the floor. That was the start of it, he says to
himself, the first mishap of the day, which led to all the others
on this day of endless mishaps, but as he continues to look at
the blackened aluminum pot on the other side of the room,
his thoughts slowly drift away from the dumb-show pratfalls
of this morning to the past, the far past flickering at the outer
edge of memory, and bit by lilliputian bit it all comes back
to him, the lost world of Then, and there he is in his barely

finished twenty-year-old body, a piss-poor, first-year graduate student on the upper Upper West Side of Manhattan marching out into the light of a late September afternoon in search of some things for the first solo apartment he has ever lived in, off to the Goodwill store on Amsterdam Avenue to buy a cupboard's worth of cheap, secondhand cooking utensils for his microscopic kitchenette, and that blank but cluttered place with the yellowed walls and dim fluorescent lights was where he caught his first glimpse of Anna, the girl with the brilliant, all-seeing eyes, no more than eighteen years old herself and a student in the neighborhood as well. Not one word exchanged between them, no more than a couple of glances in each other's direction, sizing each other up, testing out the potential pros and cons of what might or might not begin to happen if something began to happen, a little smile from her, a little smile from him, but that was all, and off she went into the September afternoon as Mr. Timid stood there like the dolt he was and still is and wound up buying this crummy aluminum pot, which cost all of ten cents and stayed with him all these years until it was finally extinguished this morning.

Eight months went by until he ran into her again, but of course he remembered her, and for reasons that are still unfathomable to him, she remembered him as well, and then it started, little by little it started until they were married five years later and his true life began, his one and only life that lasted until she ran into the Cape Cod surf nine summers ago and encountered the fierce, monster wave that broke her back and killed her, and since that afternoon, since that afternoon—*no*, Baumgartner says to himself, you mustn't go there now, you sorry bag of shit, suck it up and turn your eyes away from the pot, fuckhead, or I'll strangle you to death with my own two hands.

So Baumgartner turns his eyes from the pot on the floor and looks out into the backyard, which is little more than a patch of poorly tended grass and a single dogwood tree, not yet in bloom but beginning to sprout some buds, and lo and behold, look at that, he says to himself, a robin has landed on the grass, no doubt to scope out the territory and hunt for worms, and there, look, he's found one, he's pulling it out with his beak, and then, *thwack*, he throws it onto the grass and bobs around for a few seconds to look at other things, and then, suddenly, he pounces on the worm again and shakes it around with his beak, snips off a small bite of it and then, *thwack*, he throws it onto the ground again, bounces around a little more and then dips his head one last time, snags the worm, and swallows it in a single gulp.

Baumgartner keeps his eyes fixed on the robin as it goes about its business of catching and devouring worms, for there are many of those little creatures embedded under the surface of the backyard, far more than he ever imagined there were, and by and by, as the robin goes on pulling them out of the ground, Baumgartner begins to wonder what worms taste like and how it would feel to put a writhing, living worm in your mouth and swallow it.

2

Baumgartner is working on a new idea. It is June now, and with his little book on Kierkegaard finished and his damaged knee all but painless again, he has been delving into the knotty, intractable mind-body conundrum called *phantom limb syndrome*. He suspects the idea was planted in his head back in April when Rosita told him about her father's accident with the buzz saw, for even if she hadn't known enough to provide him with any details, Baumgartner had filled in the blanks for himself, playing out the bloody scene in his mind so often over the next several hours that he felt as if he had watched the blade slice through the carpenter's flesh with his own eyes. Mercifully, Mr. Flores's two chopped-off fingers were sewn back onto his hand that same morning, but as Baumgartner has learned since then, in cases of permanent amputation nearly everyone who loses an arm or a leg will continue to feel that the missing limb is still attached to his or her body for years afterward, often accompanied by acute pain, itching, involuntary spasms, and a sense that the limb has shrunk or has been contorted into an excruciating position. Baumgartner has plowed through the medical literature on the subject with his customary diligence, studying the work of Mitchell, Sacks, Melzack, Pons, Hull, Ramachandran, Collins, Barbin, and numerous others, even though he understands that his real interest is not in the biological and/or neurological aspects of the syndrome so much as in its power to serve as a metaphor of human suffering and loss.

It is the trope Baumgartner has been searching for ever since Anna's sudden, unexpected death ten years ago, the most persuasive and compelling analogue to describe what has happened to him since that hot, windy afternoon in August 2008 when the gods saw fit to steal his wife from him in the full vigor of her still youthful self, and just like that, his limbs were ripped off his body, all four of them, arms and legs together at the same time, and if his head and heart were spared from the onslaught, it was only because the perverse, snickering gods had granted him the dubious right to go on living without her. He is a human stump now, a half man who has lost the half of himself that had made him whole, and yes, the missing limbs are still there, and they still hurt, hurt so much that he sometimes feels his body is about to catch fire and consume him on the spot.

For the first six months he lived in a state of such profound confusion that there were times when he would wake
up in the morning and forget that Anna was dead. She had
always risen earlier than he had, up and about at least forty
minutes or an hour before he managed to open his eyes, and
so he was used to climbing out of an empty bed and sleep-
walking into an empty kitchen to prepare a mug of coffee
for himself, most often accompanied by the sound of her
typewriter clacking faintly in the small room at the other end
of the ground floor or by her footsteps moving around in one
of the upstairs rooms or else by no sound at all, which only
meant that she was reading a book or looking out the window
or otherwise engaged with some silent activity elsewhere in
the house. That explains why all those grotesque lapses of
memory occurred early in the morning, before he had been
roused to full consciousness and was groggily going about his
business under the spell of old habits formed over a lifetime of
shared life with Anna, as on the morning just ten days after
the funeral when he sat down in one of the kitchen chairs with
his steaming mug of coffee and his eyes roamed downward
to a disordered pile of open magazines heaped on the table.
One page in particular was jutting out more prominently than
the others, and on it he saw what appeared to be a headline in
the *New York Review of Books* that read: "What the Weather
Is." The book under review was something called *Waters of
the World*, and the author's name was Sarah Dry.

Waters of the World—by Sarah Dry!

The combination was so unexpected and yet so crude in its childish symmetry that Baumgartner grunted forth a brief, startled laugh, slapped his hands on the table, and stood up.

Anna, get a load of this, he said, as he started walking toward the living room. You'll wet your pants with laughter.

She must have been in the living room, he reasoned, since the typewriter was silent and there were no sounds coming from the floorboards upstairs. Therefore, she was curled up on the sofa with a book, armed with a pencil in her right hand to mark the passages that interested her, and if she wasn't using the pencil at that moment, she had no doubt put it in her mouth and was absentmindedly chewing on the metal band wrapped around the stubby pink eraser. All these images passing through his head as he walked toward her in a blur of forgetfulness—and then he stepped into the empty living room and remembered. All at once, his thoughts turned back to the funeral, and there he was along with everyone else ten days ago, standing by the open grave in the heavy, blustery air brought on by the tropical storm that was advancing up the coast with ever mounting winds, gusts so strong that one of them swept his sister's hat clear off her head and sent it flying into the air, a swirling black thing that zigzagged through the sky like a demented bird until it finally came to rest in the upper branches of a tree.

The grief counselor said: You're numb. You still haven't absorbed what's happened to you.

Whatever has happened, Baumgartner replied, didn't happen to me but to Anna. She's dead because of it, and because I saw her dead body on the beach, and because I carried that dead body in my arms, I've fully absorbed what happened to her. What galls me is that she insisted on going back into the water one last time, even though the wind had picked up and the water was churning by then, with bigger and bigger waves rolling in, crashing in, but when I said to her it was getting late and we should be going back to the house, she laughed me off and sprinted toward the surf. That was Anna, a person who did what she wanted whenever she wanted to and wouldn't take no for an answer, a person of impulse and high spirits, and a crackerjack swimmer to boot.

You blame yourself, the counselor said. That's what you seem to be telling me.

No, I don't blame myself. It would have been useless to insist. She wasn't someone you could push around or give orders to. She was a grown-up, not a child, and her grown-up decision was that she was going back into the water, and I wasn't about to stop her. I didn't have the right.

If not blame, then, a feeling of regret, even remorse.

No, and no again. I can see from your face that you think I'm resisting you, but I'm not. It's just that we need to get our terms straight before we plunge in and start to talk. Yes, she would still be alive if she hadn't gone back into the water, but then we wouldn't have lasted together for more than thirty years if I had done things like trying to stop her from going into the water when she wanted to. Life is dangerous, Marion, and anything can happen to us at any moment. You know that, I know that, everyone knows that—and if they don't, well, they haven't been paying attention, and if you don't pay attention, you're not fully alive.

How do you feel now, at this moment?

Wretched, miserable. Hammered into a thousand pieces.

In other words, dissociated, not quite yourself.

I suppose so. But to the degree that I'm able to understand what I'm going through just now, I can honestly say that I don't feel sorry for myself, and I'm not wallowing in self-pity or moaning to the heavens: Why me? Why *not* me? People die. They die young, they die old, and they die at fifty-eight. I miss her, that's all. She was the one person in the world I've ever loved, and now I have to find a way to go on living without her.

That night ten years ago, following his first and last session with Marion the grief counselor, Baumgartner went into Anna's small ground-floor study and spent several hours looking through her papers and manuscripts. The closet was stuffed from floor to chin with the drafts and proofs of her published translations, at least fifteen or sixteen books over the past twenty-five years, mostly from French and Spanish but a couple from Portuguese as well, roughly the same number of novels as collections of poems, all of which he had read two or three times and knew intimately, so he shut the closet door and moved on to the filing cabinet in a corner of the room, four deep and ample drawers that held her own writings in various stages of completion, a bulging stack of poems dating back to high school and marching forward until just three weeks before she drowned, hand-corrected typescripts of two aborted novels, several short stories, a dozen book reviews, and a medium-sized box of autobiographical writings sitting alone in the bottom drawer. Baumgartner picked up the box, carried it over to her desk, sat down in her chair, and lifted off the cover. The piece at the top of the pile was held together with a rusting paper clip, which meant that it was old, something that had been written years and years before, perhaps in the early days of their marriage, perhaps even earlier than that. He took it in his hands and began to read.

FRANKIE BOYLE

Back in the pre-dawn era of childhood, the pipsqueak years of five and six and seven and eight, baseball was my sport and I ran with the boys, a position I had to fight my way into by bloodying the nose of Marvin Howells, the lead dog of the pack, and once I had earned the respect of the gang and was allowed to take part in the after-school and weekend pickup games, I showed myself to be as good as any of them and better than most, for back in the days of my little-girl androgynous glory, I could run faster than any of them and found my spot as center fielder for all the teams I played on. Beyond the quickness of my legs and feet, my arm was more than adequate, for I was a girl who did not throw like a girl but a boy, and while I still lacked the muscle to hit with any kind of power, I banged out single after single and an occasional double in the gap, so many singles that I was rarely not on base, which fixed my role as leadoff man and prime instigator of crooked-number innings. Then we all turned nine, and the lords of ignorance dealt me my first rude slap in the face. We were old enough to join the Little League now, our first shot at organized baseball after years of playing in public parks and random backyards, a bright new world of regulation fields, team uniforms, coaches, umpires, and grandstands for spectators, a miniature version of the real thing, but according to the rules of the time, the medieval rules that lasted too long for me to benefit from their eradication, the Little League was for boys only, and therefore the fleet-footed, spray-hitting center fielder was barred from entering that enchanted realm, and her short career in the Great American Game was over.

Tough noogies, as we used to say back then, but I took the disappointment hard and sulked about it far longer than I should have, off and on for the better part of a year, with the only spiritual consolation to be found in the coed gym classes that continued until the end of elementary school, that is, until we were eleven and twelve, the coed

softball games and dodgeball games in which I still held
my own against the anointed ones with their puny dicks
and spanking white Little League uniforms, the lucky
boys who had turned against me by then and were out to
prove that I was indeed a worthless, no-account female
nothing, and how good it felt to run down their line
drives in left-center field and rob them of their sure base
hits, followed by the even greater pleasure of watching
them throw up their hands in stunned outrage as I calmly
tossed the ball back to the infield, or, in wet weather
and in winter, when we played indoors, how satisfying
it was to smash them in the face with one of my wicked
dodgeball crushers, once even to the point of bloodying
the nose of the same Marvin Howells whose nose I had
bloodied in earlier days. Best of all, because most rewarding of all, there were the after-school challenge races, the
times when I dared them to take me on in the sixty-yard
dash, one-on-one competitions out in the playground
after the three o'clock bell, a girl against a boy with a
crowd of other boys watching. For the first two years, I
never failed to win, and so confident did those victories
make me that I arrived at the erroneous conclusion that
my swiftness was eternal, but then came the third year, and
along came a certain Frankie Boyle, a lean and sparkling
young gentleman of impeccable virtue, the only male in
the class who had not turned against me and was still
my friend, and although I had bested him twice before

in similar races, Frankie had gone through a remarkable growth spurt over the summer, to such an extent that when our sixth-grade year began the boy who had once been a little shorter than I was now stood three or four inches taller than the tallest I could make myself, and there we were out in the playground on that bright September afternoon two days after the first day of school, with the customary gang of boys standing by to cheer on their man, and this time I lost, lost fair and square as Frankie Boyle sprinted past me by the seventh or eighth stride and then increased his lead all the way to the finish, so far ahead when it was over that I must have come in more than a full second behind him. There was much rejoicing in the crowd, I remember, followed by a succession of stinging taunts—*Has-been, has-been* being one, *The bitch bites the dust* being another—but to Frankie Boyle's infinite credit, for his was a soul of boundless compassion, he did not stop to bask in the cheers of the other boys but put his arm around my shoulder (the first time a boy had ever done that) and led me away from the school grounds, quietly explaining as we walked along together that it hadn't been a fair race because he was so much bigger and stronger than I was now, which had turned him into a heavyweight while I was still a welterweight, and who had ever heard of a welterweight knocking out a heavyweight, but pound for pound, he said, I was the best runner in the school, the best girl runner in all of New Jersey, and if I wanted to train for the Olympics when I was old enough to try out for the American team, he would be my trainer and make me so good and so fast that I would run away with the gold medal in world-record time. It was probably the nicest thing anyone had ever said to me, but I knew when I was licked, and I understood that my defeat in the schoolyard that day was an omen of more defeats in the months ahead. Rather than sit around and mope about my diminishing powers, I quietly withdrew from those girl-on-boy challenge sprints and sought out new activities to satisfy my craving for motion, which my restless, agitated body seemed to demand in large, regular doses, so I shifted my internal gears and went to all the weekend parties, where I danced my head off like a lunatic savage until I was the last person standing on the floor, or else I jumped into lakes and pools and oceans and swam in what I now fondly remember as *a passionate solitude*, thinking about precisely nothing but the next stroke and the next one after that as my mind emptied out and I sank into a trance that severed me from myself and made me one with the water. Weightless and alone, gliding along in my one-piece bathing suit with my flat chest beginning to swell with the first signs of the changes to come, neither here nor there nor anywhere else in the weird world turning around me.

As for sweet Frankie Boyle, I tumbled hard for him the instant he wrapped his hand around my shoulder and led me away from the school. It was the hand that did it, the jolt of electric current that buzzed through my body when his body touched mine, a sensation that was prolonged by the steady pressure of his arm against my back as his hand remained tightly fixed on my shoulder and he said all those soothing and outlandish things to buck me up and help me survive my dethronement as king of the sixty-yard dash and, in the process, turn me into the queen of all distances. Not only did I fall in love with him that afternoon, but I continued to love him all through the sixth grade, even though his strict parents refused to allow him to go to any of the weekend parties, which severely limited our chances of ever being alone together for the intense kissing and hugging sessions we both craved but only managed to indulge in three or four times because we were always surrounded by other kids. After graduating from elementary school at the end of the year, we all dispersed for the summer, and when things started up again in the fall, I moved on to the public junior high with most of our classmates, but Frankie was no longer with us. His parents had sent him off to Catholic school, and to make matters even worse, the school was several towns away in distant South Orange, *Our Lady of Sorrows*, which had to be the worst name ever invented for a school, even if it aptly expressed the sorrow I felt when Frankie called and broke the news to me. We talked on the phone a few more times that

September, mostly awkward conversations in which we didn't have much to say to each other beyond lamenting how grim and hopeless the world had become, but given that we were no more than children at the time, and given that neither one of us was a part of the other's day-to-day life anymore, the telephone calls eventually stopped.

We lost contact for several years after that, but midway through our junior year of high school there he was again, standing outside his father's gas station at the edge of town, where he had recently started working on Saturday mornings and Sunday afternoons, seventeen years old now, and tall and broad-shouldered and sweet-faced as ever. Our friendship picked up again as if the four-and-a-half-year interruption had gone by in fourteen ticks of the clock, which sounds strange but wasn't strange at all. It was true that I had kissed many boys by then and had lost my virginity to one of them, and it was also true that Frankie had the kindness that first morning to show me a picture of his girlfriend, whom he fully intended to marry one day, thus gently and ever so gracefully telling me he was off-limits, but young Mr. Boyle was the same shining person he had always been, and my soft spot for him was just as soft as it had been in the days of my welterweight past, so I flirted with him whenever I stopped by on the weekends and he flirted back, calling me Red (because of my reddish-brown hair) while I called him Flash (as in the Fordham Flash, the nickname of another Frankie, the old second baseman Frankie Frisch). The jocular, nonsensical give-and-take of childhood pals, but enjoyable for all that, since we were no longer strictly children and were growing up fast.

Frankie's duties at Boyle's Gas & Auto Repair weren't too strenuous, mostly wiping down windshields, pumping high-octane and regular into fuel tanks, and checking oil gauges and the air pressure in tires. I didn't make a regular habit of visiting him that first spring after we reconnected, perhaps once every second or third week, but I always did my best to turn up just before his shift was about to end, so that on the days when he had nothing planned for the hours after work we could cruise around in my mother's car for a while and talk. It's hard to remember exactly what we said to each other, but I can call back certain bits of conversations about such things as Albert Camus and the Beatles versus the Stones and the Six-Day War in Israel and, even though Frankie came from a hard-line, conservative family with an army vet father who had fought in the Battle of Anzio and was all in behind the Vietnam War, Frankie was against it, as I was, which helped form yet another bond between us.

It was a terrible time to be young, especially if you were a young boy approaching eighteen and the end of high school, and especially just then, in the second half of 1967 and the first half of 1968, when everything on the home front was cracking into pieces and the draft boards were going at full tilt, sucking up tens of thousands of adolescent boys and shipping them off to fight in distant jungles for no particular reason that any of them could make sense of. That was our senior year, with one of us slogging away at Livingston High School and the other at Seton Hall Prep, and to add to Frankie's confusion in the early months of '68, with Johnson announcing he wouldn't run for another term and Martin Luther King getting shot down in Memphis and scores of cities around the country on fire, his girlfriend of the past three years, Mary Ellen Something, saw fit to break up with him in May, calling Frankie a gloomy bore who no longer resembled the boy she had once loved, and on top of that there were the ever more contentious battles with his father, who started calling him a coward and a communist for opposing the war and over his dead body would he give him a single dime for college if he didn't shape up and get with the program. It was in the midst of all those roiling messes that Frankie and I latched on to each other and had our one brief fling, in the weeks between the murder of Bobby Kennedy and the end of high school, precisely four desperate but delicious all-naked love binges in the back seat of my mother's Buick, which we parked deep in the woods of the South Mountain Reservation where not even the owls could see us. Happy as I was to be in Frankie's arms, I understood that we wouldn't be walking down a long road together, that sooner rather than later circumstances would pull us apart again, which made it all the more urgent to cling to each other now and hold on for dear life.

But Frankie kept spinning, and before long he began to lose his balance. He had been accepted by three or four colleges by then, one of them being Rutgers, the state university, where the tuition was fairly low, so that even if his father made good on his promise and refused to spring for it, Frankie would be able to get by with a student loan or a scholarship or an on-campus job or a combination of all those things, which would allow him to enroll as a matriculating student in good standing, which in turn would qualify him for a deferment from the army for the next four years. It was the only sensible decision that a young person opposed to the war could make at the time, and for most of the spring he talked as if that was what he was planning to do, but then, from one day to the next, it wasn't.

He never fully explained his change of heart to me, or couldn't, or wouldn't, or never clearly understood it himself, but after thinking about it long and hard in the years since then, I believe that Frankie was in a rage against his father, who had been attacking him relentlessly for the past two years as a pansy weakling and a spineless, anti-American mama's boy, which was more than just a crudely expressed political opinion but an out-and-out assault on

Frankie's manhood, and as a proud young man who had grown to despise his father for his imbecilic cruelty but who was nevertheless too polite and too decent to turn on that father and tell him to shut up, he shut him up by electing to join the army, which he was intending to do the day after he graduated from high school. Frank, Sr., was no doubt delighted by his son's decision, but the cold fact was that Frankie hadn't done it to please his father but to spite him, to spit on him, even if he himself was only dimly aware of what he was doing.

How I wept, and how I pleaded with him, and how I carried on over the days that followed, but for all my unhinged theatrics, nothing I said did any good. Frankie was strangely at peace with himself, and right up to the moment when he walked into the local recruitment center and took the pledge, he floated along in an expansive, buoyant mood, as if the piano he had been carrying on his back for the past two years had mysteriously vanished and he could move around freely again, unburdened by doubts and second thoughts and the bitterness that had come from bearing such a heavy load.

"It's not so bad when you stop and think about it," he said. "Give two years of my life to Uncle Sam, and in return I get four years of college on the G.I. Bill, which means that I'll be in charge of myself and won't have to beg my father for the tuition." All well and good, I said, but what happens when they drop you into the jungle and a squadron of invisible men start firing bullets at you? "Not to worry," he said, breaking into a big smile. "If I could outrun the magnificent Anna Blume when I was eleven, I'll be more than fast enough to outrun those bullets now."

Frankie Boyle never made it to the jungles of Vietnam. Five weeks after he enlisted, he was involved in a mishap during a basic-training exercise at Fort Dix when a rocket launcher misfired and blew up in his hands. The explosion tore his body apart and turned it into a mass of spinning, airborne fragments that scattered in all directions before falling back to earth. When the ambulance crew arrived to look for the scattered pieces, they combed the area for more than two hours, collecting bits of fingers and toes, of arms and legs, of hands and feet, along with numerous unidentifiable shards of seared flesh and splintered bones, but with the sun beginning to sink toward the horizon and darkness coming on, they finally had to abandon the search. In spite of their efforts, there was so little left of Frankie Boyle on the day they buried him that the contents of his coffin weighed just sixty-one pounds.

Baumgartner knew about this. As far back as his earliest conversations with Anna in 1969, she had talked about Frankie Boyle and revisited the horror of his ghastly annihilation, which had cut through her like a sword, she said, and left a *permanent gash in her soul*. She had also told him that when word came to her about what had happened at Fort Dix, she had sat in her freshman dorm room at Barnard and *sobbed her heart out* for ten straight hours, sobbing as she had never sobbed before and never would again, since to sob that hard and for that long comes close to destroying you, and a body is not constructed to bear up to convulsions of that magnitude more than once in a lifetime. She hadn't touched on that episode in her piece, and for that matter the piece itself had nothing in it that was essentially new to him, but in spite of that, and far more important than that, it had stirred him deeply to see those girlhood memories dancing across the pages of her yellowed manuscript, for once he began to read her words, he felt as if he was hearing Anna's voice rise up from the paper and that she was actually talking to him again, even though she was dead now, gone now, and would never say another word to him for the rest of his life.

Baumgartner swiveled the chair to his left and began looking at Anna's old manual typewriter. The machine was perched on a sliding wooden plank that jutted from a one-inch rectangular slot just under the surface of the desk, a massive, dark-mahogany relic from the nineteen thirties or forties that she had bought for sixty dollars at a secondhand furniture place on Columbus Avenue a week before they left New York and moved into the house on Poe Road in Princeton. The typewriter had been given to her by her parents on her fifteenth birthday—May 7, 1965—and she had gone on using the dark-gray/pale-green Smith Corona portable to the end, barring a brief pause when she took a stab at switching over to a desktop computer and discovered that she didn't like it, mostly because the touch of the keyboard was too soft and made her fingers ache, she said, whereas pounding on the more resistant keys of her portable built up the strength of her hands, so she ditched the Mac by passing it on to the sixteen-year-old son of her oldest first cousin and returned to the tactile pleasures of rolling sheets of paper into the Smith Corona and filling her room with loud woodpecker music. It would seep through the walls and up through the ceiling, faintly drifting into all parts of the house, and wherever Baumgartner happened to be, he loved listening to those muted firecracker sounds, whether he was roaming in and out of the first-floor rooms or sitting in his upstairs study bent over his own writing contraption, which in his case had become a computer because it had to be a computer, since he worked at a university and his department along with all the other departments and administrative offices had gone digital. As an independent translator and free-lance writer, Anna was her own boss and could conduct her business how and where she pleased, which meant communicating by letter, phone, and fax rather than by email and continuing to do her work with the assistance of her well-worn but indestructible companion. Thank God for that, Baumgartner said to himself, and thank God for all those beautiful morning sonatas when he had woken up to the sound of Anna's fingers hammering the keys, that is, to the sound of Anna's mind singing through her fingers as they hammered the keys, and after one month of living alone in the empty house, he had come to miss those sounds so much that he would sometimes go into her room, sit down behind the silent machine, and type out something—anything—just to hear them again.

So it went for the first six months, a fissure in time that Baumgartner would later refer to as *The Vanishing*, or *Man Crazy with Grief*. For half a year he was more or less unrecognizable to himself, a being other than the one he had known and inhabited since boyhood, and in that interim zone of lost bearings and irrational impulses, he wobbled through his days by busying himself with any number of bizarre, half-cocked pursuits. Not just banging out gibberish on Anna's typewriter but squandering two entire evenings folding and refolding the things in her bureau drawers—lace panties, cotton panties, bras, camisoles, stockings, pantyhose, socks, workout shorts, tennis shorts, bathing suits, T-shirts—and aligning them in neatly ordered rows before placing each stacked pile into the drawers again, or buying expensive wooden hangers to replace the metal and plastic ones and then rehanging Anna's dresses, skirts, blouses, silk pants, woolen pants, cotton pants, hoodies, jackets, and jeans in the closet as well as buying half a dozen transparent, zippered containers for storing her sweaters on the shelf above, or pouring a mug of coffee for her every morning when he sat down at the kitchen table to drink his own mug of coffee, which he would raise in salute to her before taking the first sip, or writing several dozen pornographic love letters to her and sending them through the mail, going to the absurd trouble of folding them into envelopes, addressing them, affixing a stamp to them, and dropping them into a mailbox, followed by the pleasure of receiving them a day or two later and imagining the pleasure Anna would have felt if she had been there to receive them herself.

It probably didn't help that he had been on leave for the fall semester that year, but the hiatus had been in the works for some time, and he and Anna had arranged to spend those four-plus months of no classes in Paris, a city they had both lived in before and had been longing to live in again, even if it was for only a few months. An apartment had been rented, the round-trip tickets had been booked, and they had been planning to take off on August twentieth, two days after returning from a weeklong visit with old friends on the Cape. Instead of flying across the Atlantic with Anna on the twentieth, however, Baumgartner found himself standing next to an open grave in Princeton, New Jersey, watching a machine lower her coffin into the ground as a fierce wind crashed into his face and his friend Jim Freeman wrapped his right arm around his body to make sure he didn't fall down—a precautionary measure that had nothing to do with the wind but because it looked as if Baumgartner's legs were about to give way, and if they did, there was every chance he would topple into the grave himself.

No teaching duties, then, and therefore no responsibilities, no impingements on his time, and no pressing need to budge from his house. As far as the university was concerned, he was officially absent, and even though he stayed put and didn't leave town during that absence, he could just as well have been in Paris, Parma, or Patagonia for all the administration cared. Gone but not gone, as it were, stuck, his feet glued to the floor and living in a precarious inner space that had turned him into someone with too much time on his hands, and because Baumgartner was in no condition to resume work on his book about Thoreau or to start working on anything else, that time was exceedingly long and empty, a succession of empty days that he mostly filled by folding and refolding underwear and flooding the U.S. Postal Service with a continuous stream of hot, smutty letters to a woman whose body he would never see or touch again.

Still and all, not every hour was entirely wasted on nonsensical distractions, and as he went on studying the unpublished manuscripts of the two hundred and sixteen poems Anna had written over a span of roughly forty years, he understood that the work was more than good enough to be sent out into the world. Not all of it, perhaps, but the best eighty or a hundred would make a fine book, and so Baumgartner launched himself into the project of organizing a collection of Anna's poems, which was the one tangible thing he accomplished during those lost, shapeless months, since the book was eventually published by a small but well-regarded house of the cutting-edge variety, Redwing Press, which had a capable enough distributor to sell out the first printing in eighteen months and then immediately belch forth a second printing and four years later a third. The numbers were minute, of course, but given that poetry was not a planet but a diminutive asteroid roaming through the celestial spaces of American literature, Anna had found her own little spot in the firmament.

She could have been there all along, he felt, but for some unknown, unarticulated reason, she had never lifted a finger to put her poems in circulation. It was the thing that had baffled him most about her, for in all other ways Anna was a person who stood up for herself and fought hard for what she believed in, and she knew damned well that her poems were good. Doubts, yes, despairing moments, yes, but what writer or artist doesn't live in that shifting territory between confidence and self-contempt? The proof was in the fact that she had always shared her poems with him, not because he ever asked her but because she wanted to, either reading them out loud or handing him small sheafs of six or seven at once, and again and again he had responded to her new work by saying it was time for her to get off her ass and start publishing them, which was invariably followed by a diffident shrug from Anna, who sometimes added "You're right" or "One of these days" or "We'll see," depending on her mood. Based on those scanty remarks, he felt certain, or almost certain, that she wouldn't have objected to what he was doing now, since *one of these days* had arrived, and the crackling, effervescent poet he had lived with for close to two-thirds of his life deserved to be read by someone or many someones other than the aging sack of bones that had been her husband.

The earliest poem Baumgartner decided to include had been written in September 1971, four months after Anna's twenty-first birthday and one month after she returned from a year of studying in Paris (sandwiched between two summers in Madrid), and the title of that initial work became the title of the book as a whole, *Lexicon: Selected Poems 1971–2008*. It was by no means the best of the poems, but Baumgartner loved the whimsy and strangeness of it, the ebullient zing that somehow managed to reveal both Anna herself and the spirit of her work at the same time. More than that, his memories of himself as a young man were saturated with this poem, for not only was it written at the precise moment when he was falling heels over head in love with her, it was the first poem of hers that she ever read out loud to him—with no clothes on, sitting up in bed after a glorious fuck on the bare, rumpled sheets in his old sublet on West Eighty-fifth Street.

LEXICON

The little flower was so small
it had no name
so I called my discovery
the "Splinge"
but then I thought better of it
and renamed that tiny, tiny dot
of brilliant burning red
the "How Are You Doing
Mrs. Dolittle and Where
Have You Been Keeping Yourself Lately?"

Inasmuch as the little red dot was a flower
it said nothing back to me
and therefore I will never know
if it liked the name I had given it
or not. I walked on.
When I returned the following morning
to see if the flower had grown overnight
the little red dot was gone.

Where to now Mrs. Dolittle
and if you are gone forever
would someone please tell me
why that tiny imp of a man
is grinning at me from across the street
with a microscopic red something in his buttonhole
gleaming like a lit match in the dark.

Ten years later, Baumgartner marvels at how little has changed for him since those early months of near insanity. He has pretended otherwise, of course, and once he managed to hoist himself from the ground, stand up on his feet, and start walking again, it appeared that he had made his way back into the world of the living. He resumed teaching his classes. A month later, he was tiptoeing into his work again, then diving into it again, which has led to one book, then a second book, and now a third book—more books than in any other ten-year chunk of his life. Old friendships have deepened, new friendships have been formed, and after a year of celibate quiescence marked by glum interludes of masturbation, during which he would imagine he was in bed with Anna again, he started chasing after women for the first time in close to forty years. Signs of life, or apparent signs of life that have encouraged his friends to believe that Baumgartner has found a way to forge on without Anna. Even Baumgartner himself tends to believe it most of the time, but that is only because the artificial limbs he has attached to his legless, armless body have grown so familiar to him by now that he scarcely notices they are there. For all their efficiency, however, and all the aid they provide to the afflicted, those titanium appendages are dead things that feel nothing. Baumgartner still feels, still loves, still lusts, still wants to live, but the innermost part of him is dead. He has known that for the past ten years, and for the past ten years he has done everything in his power not to know it.

It all cracked apart for him on the day of the scorched pot and the tumble down the stairs. Until then, he hadn't understood how deeply divided he has been about all things connected to Anna, how all along he has been pushing her away from him and holding on to her at the same time, purging the house of all traces of her and yet keeping her workroom intact, giving away the voluminous assemblage of clothing he had restacked and rehung with such methodical care during his post-death meltdown and then going on to replace the bed, the stove, the refrigerator, the table and chairs in the kitchen, the living room furniture, the sheets, the pillows, the towels, the silverware, the plates, the bowls, the cups, the mugs, the drinking glasses, the teapot, the coffee maker, and a thousand other small and large things in every upstairs and downstairs room but one, and yet, even if he seldom goes into that room anymore, she is still there in the house with him, lurking somewhere close by, at times exceedingly close, but always just beyond the frame of his vision, and then she burst in on him that miserable afternoon in April as he sat at the kitchen table looking at the blackened egg boiler on the floor, the one thing he hadn't bothered to get rid of, and rather than welcome the chance to spend some time drifting along with Anna, he had kicked her away, expelling her with such brutal, unthinking vehemence that he was appalled by what he had done. Then came the spectacle of the robin devouring worms in the yard, and then came the crack, for it was only then, after nine years and eight months of struggling to live between two contradictory and mutually destructive states of mind, that he understood how thoroughly he had bungled the whole business. To live is to feel pain, he told himself, and to live in fear of pain is to refuse to live.

Two months later, he is buried in his essay on phantom limb syndrome, which he has taken to calling phantom person syndrome as the metaphorical congruencies become ever more apparent to him. He has no idea where he is going with it at this point, and he doubts he will even finish it, but for now it is filling a need, which is motivation enough for him to carry on with his research into brain maps, sense receptors, and neural circuitry in an attempt to translate mental and spiritual pain into the language of the body. He thinks of mothers and fathers mourning their dead children, children mourning their dead parents, women mourning their dead husbands, men mourning their dead wives and how closely their suffering resembles the aftereffects of an amputation, for the missing leg or arm was once attached to a living body, and the missing person was once attached to another living person, and if you are the one who lives on, you will discover that the amputated part of you, the phantom part of you, can still be a source of profound, unholy pain. Certain remedies can sometimes alleviate the symptoms, but there is no ultimate cure.

It is pushing midnight. Baumgartner has been stretched out in bed for the past hour, ready for sleep but still sleepless as he lies in the dark pondering his essay and where he is planning to go with it tomorrow morning. Little by little, however, his thoughts have begun to break apart and scatter into smaller and smaller fragments of thought as the muscles in his neck and shoulders unknot themselves and melt into the slowly dissolving muscles of his arms and legs and back. He is asleep now but does not know it. He imagines that he is only on the verge of sleep and therefore has not lost touch with his surroundings. He knows that the bed he is lying in is his bed, and that the bed is in his bedroom, and that the bedroom is in his house, the same house he lived in with Anna for twenty-four years and now lives in alone. She died on August 16, 2008, and today is June 20, 2018, or, if midnight has already come and gone, June twenty-first. Baumgartner hears a noise somewhere in the house, most likely in one of the downstairs rooms, a faint buzzing sound that lasts for a few seconds, then stops for a second, then starts again for a few seconds, then stops again for a second, an alternating pulse of sound followed by silence followed by sound, a sequence of longer sounds and shorter silences that goes on through ten or twelve repetitions and then stops. By that time, Baumgartner has already switched on the bedside lamp, rolled out of bed, and covered his naked body with his belted plaid bathrobe. The sounds are unusual enough to warrant investigation, and even if they have stopped by now, Baumgartner continues on his way to the first floor, turning on the light in the hall, going down the stairs, turning on the light in the lower hall, then the light in the living room, where he detects no signs of disturbance or intrusion, and then the light in the kitchen, where everything is precisely as he left it before going upstairs at ten, even down to the encrusted, water-filled pot in the sink, which he left to soak overnight before tackling it again in the morning.

Last of all, there is Anna's workroom, which Baumgartner fears could be vulnerable to a break-in or other sorts of mischief because of the glass-paneled door that opens directly onto the backyard. However little he goes into that room himself these days, Mrs. Flores marches in there for thirty or forty minutes every other Tuesday to vacuum, mop, and dust, conscientiously following Baumgartner's instructions to keep the place clean and in *tip-top order*. When he switches on the overhead light, Baumgartner is heartened to see that the backyard door is shut and the glass panels are unbroken. More than that, everything inside the room seems to be in its proper place. Nevertheless, feeling alert now and not the least bit tired anymore, Baumgartner opts to stay where he is rather than go back upstairs and crawl into bed—just to make sure that nothing is missing.

Anna's typewriter is still perched on the mahogany plank jutting from the desk. Her pencils and pens are still wedged into the New York Mets cup that stands a couple of inches north of the green blotter. The two objects she used as paperweights are still on the blotter itself, one in the upper left-hand corner and one in the upper right: a lump of misshapen concrete from the Berlin Wall that was given to her by a German friend in 1989; the ridged shard of an ammonite fossil more than a million years old that she accidentally kicked up from the ground during a long-ago trek through the Ardèche in south-central France. And then there is her red telephone, which is still sitting in its place southeast of the blotter, even though the service on that private line has been discontinued and the phone will never ring again.

The closet is still crammed with boxes of her translation work, and her other manuscripts are still in the filing cabinet that stands at the far end of the wall to the right of the desk. Next to the filing cabinet is the wooden bookcase, three shelves spanning about five feet with spillover books stacked on top, crotch-high for the six-one Baumgartner and waist-high for the five-eight Anna. Next to the bookcase in the near corner of the wall is the unplugged fax machine, dozing in silence on top of a narrow typewriting table with both extension wings down, each one hanging parallel to the legs. Above those three things standing on the floor, the upper parts of the wall are densely covered with framed and unframed objects, none of which has been tampered with or removed, a dozen small canvases and drawings by various friends, portraits and photographs of beloved exemplars (Emily Dickinson and Emma Goldman among them), Anna's 1997 PEN Translation Award for her *Selected Poems of Fernando Pessoa*, a movie still from *Blonde Crazy* of Joan

Blondell slugging James Cagney in the jaw, a framed square of sketchbook paper inscribed with the words of a line from another one of Blondell's films, *Dames*, "I have seventeen cents and the clothes I stand in—but there's life in the old girl yet," the original cover of Baumgartner's first published book, *The Embodied Self* (1976), and a strip of four photo booth pictures of the two of them wrapped in each other's arms and kissing madly on one of their first dates.

Baumgartner smiles at the two sexed-up kids in those grainy, black-and-white photos, then, with a theatrical flourish, bows his head in homage to the lost country of youth. He is glad that nothing has been disturbed, that the wall and the room and all the other rooms are still as they were when he climbed into bed for the night. On the other hand, if no one has broken into the house, how to explain the mysterious sounds that drove him from his bed and into this downstairs room? Is it possible that the sounds were coming from next door? Is it possible that he only imagined them? He had been straddling the borderland between wakefulness and sleep, after all, and in that hypnagogic state when the mind becomes a three-ring circus of weird, hallucinatory images, perhaps he hallucinated a sound as well. Not likely, he thinks, given the complexity of the sounds he heard, but not beyond the realm of the possible.

Baumgartner sits down in the chair behind the desk. A moment after he has settled his ass into a comfortable position, the telephone rings. The red telephone. The disconnected telephone that cannot ring but nevertheless has rung and is continuing to ring still.

Both frightened and curious, Baumgartner understands that the sounds from the ringing phone are the same sounds he heard while lying in his bed upstairs, the same alternating sequence of longer and shorter intervals of sound and silence, faint and muffled on the second floor but loud and clear on the first, and if that is the case, then whatever person or prankster or invisible agent had called earlier is now calling again.

Baumgartner lifts the receiver off the hook and hazards an uncertain, bewildered hello—a hello with a question mark attached to it. A silence follows, during which he tells himself that he must be dreaming, even though he is awake and cannot be dreaming, and then Anna is talking to him, talking to him with the same resonant voice that belonged to her when she was alive, addressing him as *darling* and *my darling man*, explaining to him that death is not what anyone had ever imagined it was, that the two of them and all the other materialists had been wrong to assume there is no afterlife but that the afterlifes of the Christians, the Jews, the Muslims, the Hindus, the Buddhists, and all the others have gotten it wrong as well. There are no divine punishments or rewards, no trumpets or fires of perdition, no bowers of heavenly bliss, and no human being will ever go back to earth as a butterfly, a crocodile, or the next incarnation of Marilyn Monroe. What happens after death is that you enter the Great Nowhere, a black space in which nothing is visible, a soundless vacuum of nullity, the oblivion of the void. There is no contact with any other dead person, and no ambassador from on high or down low comes to brief you on what will be happening next. She therefore has no idea how long her present condition will last, if *present* is a relevant term anymore in a place such as this one, which is not even a place but a nowhere, a blank null subtracted from an infinity of nulls. She sees nothing and hears nothing because she has no body anymore, no *extension* as the old philosophers used to put it, which means that she is never tired or hungry or feels any pain or pleasure or anything at all, and if she could be measured in space, if such a term as *space* is relevant anymore, she is probably no bigger than a subatomic particle, the merest, most minuscule fraction of the cosmic What. Call her a What, if he likes, or a spirit, or an emanation of the vast, formless surround, or, quite simply, a monad that thinks, and when she thinks it sometimes happens that she can see the things she is imagining, see them clearly in her mind's eye, if she had such things as a mind or an eye anymore, which she doesn't, but nevertheless she can see them clearly, almost as clearly as she once did when she was alive on earth.

Baumgartner says nothing. He wants to talk, he wants to tell her a hundred things and ask her a hundred questions, but he seems to have lost the power to open his mouth and speak. No matter, he says to himself. The call could end abruptly at any moment, and why bother to talk when all he wants is to go on listening to Anna's voice until the time runs out and she vanishes into the darkness again?

She can't be sure of anything, she says, but she suspects that he is the one who is sustaining her through this incomprehensible afterlife, this paradoxical state of conscious non-existence, which must and will come to an end at some point, she feels, but as long as he is alive and still able to think about her, her consciousness will continue to be awakened and reawakened by his thoughts, to such an extent that she can sometimes go into his head and hear those thoughts and see what he is seeing through his eyes. She has no idea how this happens, nor does she understand why she is able to talk to him now, but the one thing she does know is that the living and the dead are connected, and to be as deeply connected as they were when she was alive can continue even in death, for if one dies before the other, the living one can keep the dead one going in a sort of temporary limbo between life and not-life, but when the living one also dies, that is the end of it, and the dead one's consciousness is extinguished forever. Anna pauses for a moment to take in her breath, and then, breathing out again, she asks a question for the first time since he picked up the phone: Does any of this make sense to you? Before Baumgartner can answer her, Anna's breathing stops, her words stop, and the line goes dead.

3

After Baumgartner dreams that dream, something begins to change in him. He is fully aware that the
disconnected telephone did not ring, that he did not hear
Anna's voice, that the dead do not go on living in a state of
conscious non-existence, and yet however unreal the contents
of the dream might have been, he experienced them as a real
experience, and the things he lived through in his sleep that
night have not vanished from his thoughts as most dreams
do. Six days have passed since then. Short as that time has
been, Baumgartner feels as if he has been thrust into a
new internal space and that the circumstances of his life
have been altered. He is no longer trapped in a windowless,
subterranean chamber but is somewhere aboveground, still
stuck in a room, perhaps, but at least this one has a barred
window at the top of the outer wall, which means that light
pours in during the day, and if he stretches out on the floor

and places his head at the correct angle, he can look up and study the clouds as they float past him in the sky. Such is the power of the imagination, he tells himself. Or, quite simply, the power of dreams. In the same way that a person can be transformed by the imaginary events recounted in a work of fiction, Baumgartner has been transformed by the story he told himself in the dream. And if the windowless room now has a window in it, who knows if a day won't come in the not too distant future when the bars will have vanished and he will at last be able to crawl out into the open air.

It would be absurd to believe that his thoughts are sustaining Anna in some disembodied, etherealized afterlife, that simply keeping himself alive on earth has allowed her to maintain contact with him from her subatomic outpost in the Great Nowhere, but given that he was the author of those absurdities himself, he cannot dismiss them out of hand or pretend they have not offered him some measure of spiritual comfort, for the fact is that he has never not been in contact with Anna since the day she drowned, and if he has now conjured up an alternative world in which she knows that he is thinking about her, can feel him thinking about her, can think about him thinking about her, who is to say there isn't some truth to it? Not a scientific truth, perhaps, not a verifiable truth, but an emotional truth, which in the long run is the only thing that counts—what our man feels, and how he feels in relation to those feelings. S.T. Baumgartner, noted author of nine books and numerous shorter works on philosophical, aesthetic, and political matters, beloved member of the Princeton faculty for the past thirty-four years, an aging phenomenologist who has spent his life in the realm of the tangible, a lone traveler plodding waist-deep through the mysterious, ontological swamps of human perception, has finally found religion. Or what passes for religion in a man who has none and believes in nothing but the obligation to ask good questions about what it means to be alive, even if he knows he will never be able to answer them.

Six days after that, the bars in the window disappear. Before he can figure out a way to climb up and wriggle his body through the hole, the walls of the room have disappeared as well, and he finds himself standing out in the open. He is in a meadow somewhere in the middle of the country, with no houses or telephone poles or other traces of human presence anywhere in sight. Knee-high grass surrounds him on all sides, and the gray sky above him is filled with bulked-up, darkening clouds. Rain threatens to fall within a matter of minutes. He shoves his hands into his pockets and begins to walk.

And so it is that Baumgartner rediscovers the enlivening, proprioceptive pleasures of motion, the simple act of putting one foot in front of the other and propelling himself through space, the whole of his body aligned in the parallel rhythms of his thumping heart, his expanding and contracting lungs, and the steady left-right-left-right movement of his legs, and once he begins to hit his stride in the days that follow, he feels greater and greater confidence in himself as he continues to traverse the vast internal meadow that stretches on before him. Never mind that his pace is slower than it was in the past, never mind that he is occasionally pelted by downpours or pounded by harsh, jagged winds blowing in from the east, he is upright and ambulatory, and now that the cadences of his heart, lungs, and legs have been synchronized to carry him along for the long haul, Baumgartner has simultaneously achieved a new clarity of mind, an emboldened sense of his own future that he now knows must be acted upon at once—or else. He is seventy years old, after all, and the time for dithering has come to an end.

For one thing, he concludes that the moment has come for him to retire. He will withdraw from active teaching duties and take on the august if meaningless position of *professor emeritus*, relinquishing his spot in the department to a youngblood from the next generation. He will be putting himself out to pasture, as it were, but not into permanent exile, since he will be allowed to maintain his connection to the university with full library privileges and the right to go on using his Princeton email address. His many friendships with his colleagues from various departments will go on as before, and he will continue to attend lectures, discussions, and informal gatherings if and when the spirit moves him, but all the burdensome aspects of his job will suddenly and mercifully disappear: no more dreadful committee meetings, no more haggling with disgruntled students over their grades, no more bureaucratic bullshit. In other words, an unfettered, independent life—with a monthly income from his pension that will roughly match if not slightly exceed the salary he earned while on active duty. A new book has been taking shape in him over the past several months, an outlandish, off-the-wall project that is unlike anything he has attempted in the past, a serio-comic, quasi-fictional discourse on the self in relation to other selves called *Mysteries of the Wheel*, and he wants to devote as much time as possible to it, since time is of the essence now, and he has no idea how much of it he has left. Not just how many years before he kicks the bucket but, more to the point, how many years of active, productive life before his mind or his body or both begin to fail him and he is turned into a pain-racked, imbecilic incompetent, unable to read or think or write, to remember what someone just said to him four seconds ago, or to muster the oomph to get it up anymore, which is a horror he does not wish to contemplate. Five years? Ten years? Fifteen years? The days and months are rushing past him ever more quickly now, and whatever time he has left will flit by in a blink. How dreadful it would be to croak in the academic harness, hunched over his desk writing comments in the margins of yet another student paper. No, that must not be allowed to happen, and when the end comes, at least may he be granted the dignity for his heart to stop while he is pushing out one last sentence of his own, preferably the final words of a loud fuck-you addressed to the power-hungry madmen who rule the world. Or, even better than that, to give up the ghost while walking down the street on his way to a midnight rendezvous with the woman he loves.

Her name is Judith, and that is the next thing Baumgartner has decided he must act upon at once—this week, this minute, now. The dream has finally made this possible after two years of growing intimacy with her, the sudden release of Anna's hold on him after a decade of self-inflicted torment that blocked him from tumbling whole hog into any of the several liaisons he formed with the widows and divorcées who drifted in and out of his life during the years between Anna and Judith, but this time is different, this time he has fallen in love, and this time he is ready for another shot at marriage, if she will have him, of course, which is by no means certain but seems more likely than not—he hopes.

Judith now, but only because the dream has led to a new turn in his relations with Anna's ghost, which has allowed him to step back into the rooms of the past without fear of getting trapped in them anymore, and now that he has revisited those rooms and already come out of them again, he is prepared to devote his energies fully to the present, that is, to Judith, which also means that the present Baumgartner has in mind will necessarily spill over into the future—as long as the answer is yes and not no.

In anticipation of this moment, this *now*, he has spent the better part of the past three weeks submerged in the world of Then, ruminating, reminiscing, and roaming around among the forty years between his first glimpse of Anna as a girl of eighteen and his last glimpse of her as a woman of fifty-eight, dead on the beach. Strangely, he did not feel alone. Anna was at his side, and all through the journey they were walking together, talking together, each one listening and speaking to the other as they wandered in and out of the rooms and down the dimly lit corridors of the memory palace, revisiting hundreds of large and small things that had happened to them over those forty years. Needless to say, she was not with him in the flesh, but by reading through her letters and manuscripts for the first time in God knows how long, he found her voice again, and by poring over the countless photographs that he and others had taken of her throughout her life, he found her body again. Not her real body, of course, and not her real voice—but almost. For such are the powers of memory bestowed on a man who has listened to the voice of his dead wife talking to him through the disconnected wires of a defunct telephone.

From the box in the bottom drawer of the filing cabinet: Anna's last autobiographical piece, written less than a year before she died but going back into the distant past to tell the story of how and why and under what circumstances Baumgartner finally popped the question of marriage—in the wee hours of that fraught November night in 1972 that could have been the end of Anna but wasn't.

SPONTANEOUS COMBUSTION

I was in love with S. by the time I graduated from college. There was no one else I was even vaguely interested in anymore, which meant that my heart was entirely in his hands, and because S. loved me just as much as I loved him, his heart was entirely in my hands, which allowed us to think of ourselves as a couple, a pair of besotted loners who saw eye to eye on everything that mattered and had no intention of parting ways. In spite of those certainties, it never occurred to us to set up house together, and not once had either one of us breathed the word *marriage*. We were still too young to make plans, too unsettled to have formed any clear ideas about the future, and whenever we did manage to think ahead about something, I doubt those thoughts traveled much beyond the next few weeks or months. For the not yet twenty-five-year-old S., the future meant finishing up his dissertation on Merleau-Ponty by mid-spring and earning his doctorate in philosophy, after which he would decide what he wanted to do next. For the just turned twenty-two-year-old me, the future meant pushing on with my gnomic little verses and adjusting to the demands of my first full-time job, which paid all of eighty-seven dollars and fifty cents a week.

Heller Books was a new operation back then, a not yet fully born literary house that was scrambling to publish its first list of titles in the fall. The budget was tight, so tight that there were only three of us working with the twenty-eight-year-old Morris Heller that summer—a senior editor, a production manager, and myself, the youngest body on the team, serving in my double role as junior editor and personal assistant to Morris, who had hired me because translated novels were an essential part of the program and I happened to be fluent in French and Spanish. We were all on rock-bottom salaries, and every morning we commuted to a shabby office on lower West Broadway, just ten blocks north of the World Trade Center construction site and smack in the middle of the neighborhood now known as Tribeca, which at that point was still without a name. Triangle below Canal. A no-man's-land of nineteenth-century industrial buildings where a smattering of artists had set up lofts and everything went dark after five, but rents were low down there in the early seventies, the lowest rents anywhere in lower Manhattan, and Morris had to stretch his pennies as far as he could.

Thirty-five years later, I can still see the four of us toiling away at our desks in that medium-to-large-sized room lined with metal bookcases and cabinets on three of the walls, a raw, bare-to-the-bone ancient loft with a tin ceiling and a chipped wooden floor, no air-conditioning but three gargantuan windows running along the wall that faced the street, which kept us supplied with an abundance of light, and when it got hot in there during the summer, which it always did, there was nothing for it but to turn on

71

the three industrial-strength pedestal fans and wait for a hair-rumpling blast every five point two seconds. A brief but soothing respite from the dog-day sweats, but what a hideous tangle those fans wrought on the uppermost parts of a girl's head, so I marched into a hairdresser's place on the first Saturday I had off, showed the stylist a photograph of Jean Seberg in *Breathless*, then another one of Audrey Hepburn in *Roman Holiday*, and told her to split the difference between the two. Thus my locks were shorn, and when S. told me how smashing I looked with that skimpy cut, I kept it that way and have been walking around with short hair ever since.

Given our downtown address, it would have made sense for me to live somewhere within walking distance of the office, preferably in a neighborhood below Fourteenth Street, but even the crummiest rattrap in the Village was out of my price range. After three weeks of dogged searching, the best I could manage was staying put in Morningside Heights, my old haunts of the past four years and a part of town I desperately wanted to leave, but a Barnard friend was moving out of her apartment on Claremont Avenue and I replaced her, sharing those large, ugly digs with three other girls, two of them graduate students at Columbia and the other a sad-eyed, ever less hopeful aspiring actress who had a job waiting tables at a Broadway diner just a few blocks to the south. Lucky her. A job within walking distance of where she lived. Meanwhile, I was traveling back and forth on the IRT between 116th and Chambers five times a week, roughly seven miles in each direction with close to two hours of commuting time per day. The job was worth the effort, I felt, but the apartment was loathsome, a crumbling, bug-infested dump in a wrecked neighborhood crawling with junkies and an army of mad people who had been tossed out onto the streets when the mental hospitals shut down. A ragged, rough and-tumble time in the capital of the world, a.k.a. Fun City. Brick by brick, New York was dismantling itself. The public till was running dry, and from one week to the next the numbers kept mounting—more muggings, more murders, more stick-ups, more rapes. With so many needle-men in my neck of the woods, I would automatically clench my fists every time I walked past one of those jonesing scarecrows with the pinprick eyes, wondering if it wasn't finally my turn to have a switchblade pulled on me as a shaky voice announced that my throat would be slit if I didn't hand over this thing, that thing, and all the other things I was carrying *right now*.

Fortunately, there were opportunities to escape, and all through those early months as a post-graduate working girl, I spent about half my nights crashing with S. But no, even if we had wanted to move in together at that point, which we didn't, it wouldn't have been possible in that place. My beloved's micro-lodgings consisted of just one room, and as that room lacked the space for a single person to live there with any degree of comfort, long-term occupancy by two was out of the question. Imagine the happy couple sharing a cramped studio apartment with two grimy windows that looked out on a brick wall, a foam mattress mounted on nine milk crates to stand in for the nuptial bed, one desk and one chair for two people who spent the bulk of their time writing, one of whom was also a junior editor, an overloaded six-shelf bookcase, a kitchenette with a shallow metal sink, a two-burner stovetop with no oven, and a minibar fridge jammed into the space where the oven should have been, a midget table for eating, accompanied by two short stools that were stowed under the table when not in use, a closet with a horizontal pole for hangers and a squat chest of drawers just under the dangling coats and shirttails, and last of all a bathroom large enough for an old-fashioned, claw-footed bathtub and sufficient space to line one of the walls with several more towers of books. S. was under no delusions about his third-floor walkup and readily admitted that the place was *awful beyond words*, but some of the happiest hours of my life were spent in there, and whenever I think back to that time now, what I mostly see is the two of us tumbling around naked on the bed and gobbling each other up in ecstatic binges of nightly sex, or else waking up early to rush off to work while S. was still asleep and stopping to look at him sprawled out on the mattress, my brilliant, long-legged man with the rumpled hair and remarkable eyes, my comrade, my fuck-buddy, my wisecracking, true-blue companion for the long road ahead, and because I hated to leave him without saying good-bye, I would mist up the air above his body with half a dozen small blasts of my lily-of-the-valley eau de cologne so that a part of me would still be there with him when he opened his eyes.

Then came the night of Wednesday, November twenty-second, the eve of Thanksgiving and the ninth anniversary of Kennedy's murder in Dallas. After an especially long day at work, Morris sprang for a pre-holiday dinner with the staff at a French restaurant in the Village. It turned out to be a noisy, high-spirited affair that went on for three or three and a half hours, and once the merry little band of literary warriors had polished off their last sips of cognac, I headed for the subway at Sheridan Square with seven dollars and change in my purse, wondering if I should take the IRT local all the way to 116th or switch to the express at 14th and then switch back to the local at 96th—the deep thoughts of a slightly tipsy person at eleven o'clock on her way home after a fifteen-hour slog of too much work and too much food. I can't remember which train or trains I took, but I returned to my neighborhood at about a quarter to twelve. A dark November night, chill boring down into my bones, and a mist hanging in the air that veiled the streetlamps in a nimbus of dull, glowing fuzz. The moon was hidden behind the clouds, there were

no stars in the sky. Broadway and 116th Street to begin
with, then the walk down 116th on the incline toward
the river, followed by the sharp right turn at Claremont
Avenue, and the six-block walk ahead of me. A few midnight stragglers for the first couple of blocks, then no one.
A dark stretch between there and home, with nothing but
the sound of my footsteps clicking on the sidewalk as I
imagined going into the apartment and sliding into bed.
Somewhere between 119th and 120th, a man drifted out
from the shadows, swung around in a slow, lazy pivot, and
planted himself in the middle of the sidewalk, blocking my
way. Too dark, too misty to make out much of anything.
Strong or frail, old or young, impossible to know, not
even the face, which was just a few inches from mine, but
nothing more than a flash or two from the whites of his
eyes, a cryptogram of a person, a smudge in the night, but
I could smell him, could suck in the sour breath floating
out of his mouth and into my face, into my nose, and down
into my body, and then he said: "Cough it up, or this knife
goes into your gut." I heard his switchblade snap open,
and when I saw what must have been the knife going up
toward my face, everything began to slow down in my
head, and I understood or thought I understood that this
slowing down meant I was looking at my death and that
these were the last moments of my life. How many more
seconds, I wondered, and as my breath speeded up and I
breathed into his breath which was breathing into mine,

I suddenly remembered that I had put on flat shoes that morning, and if these were my last moments on earth, I said to myself, better to make a last stand and not give in, and so, rather than open up my purse and fork over my seven dollars and wait for him to stab me with his knife because the amount was too small, I turned and ran, ran for all I was worth, ran as I hadn't run since Frankie Boyle ran past me in the sixth grade, ran as I would have run if Frankie had trained me to outrun death, and off I went, sprinting down Claremont Avenue in the misty November night, running as hard as I could to escape the man with the knife, and even though I sensed he had been too startled by my sudden bolt to go after me or was too slow or too weak to make the effort, I kept on running to 116th Street and then up the hill and continued down Broadway for five or six or seven blocks, and then, pausing for a moment to catch my breath, I saw a cab speeding along in my direction, threw up my arm, and lo and behold the driver stopped. I climbed in and told him to take me to Eighty-fifth between Columbus and Amsterdam. I was sweating in my winter coat and yet shivering at the same time, both hot and cold at the same time, and I was all blank inside, without a single thought in my head.

As we approached Eighty-fifth Street, I began to fret that S. wouldn't be there. Out with his basketball buddies in some bar, maybe, or off seeing a philosopher friend, or flirting with the stacked, bleached-blonde waitress in the all-night diner on Columbus Avenue between Eighty-second and Eighty-third Streets, and when I pressed the buzzer to his apartment, I prepared myself for no response. There wasn't one. I buzzed again just to make sure, but again there was no response. I sat down on the cracked tile floor of the little entranceway, leaned my back against the wall with the buzzers and mailboxes, and closed my eyes, trying to think about my next move, but I was still too emptied out to think about anything. A good cry might help, I said to myself, and as I sat there trying to force some tears into my eyes, the door opened, and there was S., back from a late-night cigarette run. He hadn't been gone for more than ten minutes. Other than that, he had been at home all night working on his dissertation.

He was alarmed, of course, and deeply upset, and more than a little angry. I couldn't go back there, I told him, I'd had it with Claremont Avenue and 122nd Street and would start looking for another place, but what was I going to do in the meantime? Stay with him, of course, he replied, wasn't that obvious? But it's too small, I said.

"Of course it is," he said, "but it would only be for a little while, a month maybe, two at the most. In the meantime, we'll start looking for something bigger. This is only a sublet, after all, and I have to be out of here by February first anyway. We could move downtown, all the way downtown, and then you could walk to work and kiss the IRT good-bye."

"Move in together, you mean? Are you sure?"

"You could have been killed tonight, and when I think about what that would have done to me, I'm absolutely sure. More sure than ever, and I started being sure the first time I set eyes on you. So sure now, Anna, that not only do I want to live with you, I want to live with you forever."

"Forever?"

"Forever."

"Are you asking me to marry you?"

"That's it. I'm asking you to marry me. And the sooner the better."

I didn't know what to say, so I said nothing and just let that wild, unprecedented idea hang in the air as S. walked into the bathroom and turned on the faucets of the tub. What I needed was a good long soak in a hot bath, he said, and so I went in, took off my clothes, and lay down in the water with my eyes shut as S. gently washed me with a thick, smooth sponge. I remember listening to the water slosh around in the tub, but other than that there were no sounds in the apartment, no sounds in the world. Then, after what seemed to have been hours, I opened my eyes and started to laugh, and a moment after that I said yes.

Forty-six years later, as Baumgartner prepares himself to ask the marriage question for the second time in his life, his biggest worry is that Judith will turn him down because he is too old for her. With Anna, the gap between their ages had been just two and a half years. With Judith, it is sixteen, and at fifty-four she is still barreling ahead at full strength, whereas he is no longer barreling but chugging (on his best days) and at times even sputtering (on his worst). Until now, the discrepancy has not caused any serious problems in the sex department, nor any in any other department he can think of, and as far as he can tell there is nothing in the immediate, day-to-day flow of the present to threaten their attachment to each other, but a marriage proposal will add another element to the equation and necessarily push her into thinking about the future, and when she considers how life will look to her ten or twenty years from now, the prospect of sleeping beside an eighty- or ninety-year-old man could send her running for the hills. Thanks but no thanks, my fine-feathered geezer, but what on earth are you talking about? Baumgartner dreads the humiliation that could be in store for him, but at the same time he also knows that if he fails to summon the courage to ask the question, he will despise himself as a coward and slowly devolve into a bitter old man, a doddering Prufrock consumed by regret until the end of his days.

Her full name is Judith Feuer, and she teaches film studies at Princeton. She arrived on campus in the early two-thousands, long enough before the Cape Cod disaster to have formed a friendship with Anna, who was mad for old American movies of the thirties and forties and found an ideal interlocutor in Judith, who seemed to know more about those films than any other person alive, and as Judith was still married to Joseph Frederickson back then—a once promising but failed novelist who now earned his living cranking out popular but second-rate crime stuff—the two couples occasionally joined forces for restaurant dinners or little dinner parties at one or the other's house. Baumgartner liked Judith from the start, less so her husband, but what mattered to him most at the time was that she and Anna hit it off so well, since Anna had many friends but few close ones, and this one seemed to be developing into something close, but then Anna died, and that was the end of it. Judith was inordinately good to him during the early months of his meltdown—a number of long talks on the phone, impromptu visits to check in on him, which made him like her even more than he had to begin with—and the magnitude of her own grief over Anna's death somehow consoled him as well. Then she went off on a yearlong sabbatical, and by the time she returned Baumgartner had already begun his fitful, scattershot conquest of various widows and divorcées in Princeton, New Brunswick, Brooklyn, Manhattan, and once as far off as Shelter Island, a blob of land between the North and South Forks of eastern Long Island. Useless errands on a road to nowhere, but those short-term dalliances kept him busy and distracted, which was no doubt all he was looking for or capable of at the time. He remained in touch with Judith, but less intimately than before and with greater and greater intervals between contacts. Then, in 2014, burly Joe Frederickson ran off to New Mexico with a local real estate agent half his age, and Judith was suddenly in the throes of a divorce, which dragged on for more than a year. That was when she began calling him again and asking for his advice, explaining that because he'd had such a long, good marriage to someone as precious as Anna (her word, *precious*), she felt that she could count on him to steer her through the storm. Then she called him *wise*, a word that no one else had ever used in connection to him except Anna, and because he was wise, she said, she trusted him above all other people. Both flattered and discombobulated by this endorsement, Baumgartner cleared his throat several times and asked how her kids were taking it. Fortunately, Judith said, they were both on her side, and one by one they had both confessed to her that they were glad she was finally rid of *that creep* (Eric, age twenty-four, a tech boy with a job in Boulder, Colorado), and *that self-centered masculine shit* (Libby, age twenty-two, an aspiring documentary filmmaker in Berkeley). Baumgartner laughed and said, I'd say you're more than halfway home already, Judith, and when Judith laughed as well, the slow, stately dance that has led to his impending marriage proposal began.

After much thought on the subject, Baumgartner has concluded that among the many small and large differences between Anna and Judith, this one is the largest: the fact that Judith is a mother and Anna was not. Both he and Anna had wanted to make a child together, perhaps even more than one, but when the two of them got down to it in earnest about six years into their marriage, nothing happened.

With no luck after hundreds of nights and mornings and afternoons of unprotected sex from every angle and contorted position they could think of, they began consulting doctors, both separately and together, first one set, then another set, and finally a third set, all of whom concurred that neither he nor Anna was genetically equipped to make babies, an implausible but thrice-proven medical fact that would have meant childless marriages for both of them no matter what partners they had found.

It was a rough blow, without question the hardest thing they ever had to face together, but at least their disappointment could be shared, since they were equally responsible for the bad hand they had been dealt, which eliminated all possible resentments or silent recriminations and allowed them to go on loving each other as before, if not more deeply than before. They talked about adoption for an hour or two one morning, but neither of them had been terribly enthusiastic. They didn't want a stranger's baby, they decided, they wanted their own baby or none at all, and if fate had declared that it should be none at all, then what choice did they have but to accept it? Time passed, and as the years went by they turned into one of those perpetually young couples, a pair of slowly aging kids unburdened by the responsibilities and worries of most other married people, the often pitied and sometimes envied Baumgartner and Blume, the barren ones who had no children and therefore lived solely for each other and their work. It had been enough for Baumgartner, more than enough through all the years he spent with Anna, and even now, when he thinks about how different life would have been for them if they had managed to produce children, it is still enough. Not more than enough, but enough.

That is the first thing—motherhood—but there are numerous other differences as well, beginning with the radical contrast in their looks, a matter of little consequence to Baumgartner in the long run but nevertheless worth noting. Anna with her sleek swimmer's body, her small breasts and narrow hips, her long arms and elegantly squared-off shoulders, her short reddish-brown hair and burning gray-green eyes, as opposed to the softer, rounder Judith, who is wider in the hips, broader in the beam, and fuller in the chest, with dark brown eyes and abundant dark brown hair, not quite the scintillating beauty Baumgartner saw whenever he looked at Anna, but to his eyes still an alluring, deeply attractive woman, slower and more languid in her movements than the springing, high-speed Anna, with a warm, welcoming face that draws him in whenever he looks at her and holds him in her orbit, rapt and attentive, alive to her in all the ways he had once been alive to Anna. No other women have done that to him. Only Anna and Judith—which perhaps explains why he has fallen in love with both of them and has wanted to marry them and live with them until the end of his life, first one and now the other.

Different bodies, but different temperaments as well. A matter of inborn characteristics to some degree, along with how they were touched and held and cared for by their mothers as infants and fledgling tots, but also the result of how differently they responded to the almost identical circumstances of their childhoods. For a moneyless person like Baumgartner, who was born into a struggling lower-middle-class family, a part of him still gapes at the wealth and comfort that surrounded Anna and Judith when they were young. Dr. Leo Blume, born into a moneyless family himself, worked his way through medical school and turned into an ear, nose, and throat man who built such a thriving practice that in 1954 he and his wife and their only child transplanted themselves from a two-bedroom apartment in the Crown Heights section of Brooklyn to a large split-level house in the suburban town of Livingston, New Jersey, Anna's permanent address until she finished high school fourteen years later. In the splendor of that grassy, tree-filled domain, the little one was showered with all the blessings her father's money could provide: a spacious bedroom of her own, shelves and boxes overspilling with toys, piano lessons, ballet lessons, a multitude of books, top-of-the-line clothing, healthy, abundant meals, summer camps, birthday parties with custom-made cakes, a dog, another dog after the first dog died, and, in short, whatever she wanted whether she wanted it or not. Mostly, she didn't want. At least not after she was eleven or twelve and had learned how to think for herself, at which point her attitude toward the conditions of her life as a coddled child from the upper reaches of the upper-middle class began to change from one of blind complicity to sullen resistance to out-and-out rebellion. She knew that her parents loved her, and in spite of herself she knew that she loved them back, but at the same time she loathed them for having bought into the American myth that money is the measure of all things, even as they pretended to be alarmed by the misery of the impoverished millions who had been crushed under the wheels of the same system that had allowed them to emerge as so-called winners. Good for her parents, Anna thought, but she herself had nothing to do with it and wanted no part of that nonsense in the future, but for now, still trapped in the Livingston castle as a powerless, no-account teenager, there was little she could do but struggle to carve out an independent territory for herself within the kingdom ruled by her parents. Defending that turf wasn't easy, and countless battles were fought over it in the years that followed, but bit by bit she managed to train her parents to respect the boundaries she had drawn, arguing that her good grades should exempt her from all reproach, and if her view of the world happened to differ from theirs, they would just have to accept it. They were the ones who had encouraged her to read, after all, and now that she had emigrated to the country of books and was determined to become a poet, they should be glad she hadn't been derailed as so many of her friends had been in the past year or two, Debbie and Alice, for example, who had turned into pot-smoking flower children, or chubby Maureen, who spread her legs for any boy who deigned to look at her, or Angela, who had fallen in love with a dropout car thief, and weren't they the lucky ones, she would say to her parents, for having produced such a good girl.

Sometime in the early weeks of her last year of high school, with her thoughts trained ever more insistently on the future, Anna struck a bargain with them. She wanted to go to college, she said, she needed to go to college, and because she knew they wanted her to go as well and were more than willing to pay for it, she would gladly—and thankfully—accept the money it would take for them to carry her through those four years. But that would be the end of it, she announced, and from then on she would be out on her own as a fully independent adult, with no help from parents, relatives, or anyone else. Father Leo and mother Rachel responded to this declaration far more calmly than Anna had been expecting, no doubt because their intractable, pigheaded daughter was talking about something that wouldn't come up for another five years, and the odds were that she would have grown up enough by then to have changed her mind. An admirable position, her father said, addressing Anna in his most reasonable tone of voice, but what if you should fall on hard times? Do you want us to stand by and do nothing while you slowly starve to death? Anna laughed. No, of course not, she said, and with that turn in the conversation they extracted a promise from her to call them the moment she found herself in a fix. Some more haggling followed, but in the end Anna forced them to concede that the word *fix* meant *Do not break glass, except in the case of utmost dire emergency.*

They had underestimated her, of course. The five years passed, the seventeen-year-old Anna turned into the twenty-two-year-old Anna, and the day after she was handed her bachelor's degree by the Barnard College president, she stepped down from her throne as bourgeois American princess and promptly ran off to the circus. Little matter that the primary attractions of that seedy big top were the dump on Claremont Avenue, Baumgartner's even smaller dump on West Eighty-fifth Street, and her low-paying job at Heller Books—the important thing was that she was standing on her own two feet and making her own way. As Baumgartner joked to her one morning, thrusting an imaginary microphone toward her face: Miss Blume, most economists and sociologists would interpret this new, semi-proletarian life of yours to be an extreme example of accelerated downward mobility. Would you care to comment? To which Anna replied: Thank you, Mr. Baumgartner. All I have to say to the professors is this: You ain't seen nothin' yet, boys!

Then came the night of November twenty-second, which began with Anna outsprinting her run-in with death through a blur of fog and fear and ended with her exultant vow to marry Baumgartner at the first possible moment. The following afternoon, they climbed onto a bus at the Port Authority Terminal and headed out to Livingston for Thanksgiving dinner at Anna's parents' house. During the one hundred and one minutes it took them to get there, Baumgartner managed to persuade Anna that their housing dilemma qualified as a legitimate *utmost dire emergency*, since they needed to move to a larger place, and the grim fact was that they couldn't afford to move, not when signing a lease would oblige them to cough up the first month's rent, the last month's rent, and a security deposit that would amount to another month's rent—all in one go. He sympathized with her resolve not to accept handouts from her parents, and he understood the many reasons why she had cut the cord, but this was the day when they were going to announce their marriage plans to them, and in all the excitement that was bound to follow, Anna's mother would start talking about the wedding, which no doubt had been dancing around in her head for years and by now had blossomed into a full-blown, high-cost extravaganza, a wretched prospect that neither one of them had the stomach for, but one way or the other, Baumgartner said, thousands of dollars were going to be spent on them, whether they liked it or not, and therefore the one sensible thing they could do was to tell her parents not to throw away their money on a pointless, ephemeral, one-day affair but to invest that money, or at least some part of it, in their daughter and son-in-law's future, which would allow them to set up house in a decent apartment somewhere and get off to a good start together. Leave it to me, Baumgartner said. After twenty years of practice, they've learned all the tricks about how to argue with you, but they've never tangled with me, and if you let me do the talking, I think we'll have a better chance. A City Hall wedding, I'll say, with the two of them as our sole witnesses, and afterward the four of us will go out for a fabulous lunch at some posh midtown restaurant. When your mother objects and tells us how disappointed she is, nay, utterly heartbroken and despondent, I'll revive her spirits by suggesting they throw a party for us about two weeks later, a Sunday afternoon thing at their house, which will cost them about one one-thousandth of what a big wedding would have cost, what they call an open house, I believe, where they can show you off in your tight, sexy, black cocktail dress to your two grandmothers and five aunts and four uncles and twelve cousins and a few dozen of their friends, and once I've concluded my little spiel, your good-hearted, practical father will turn to your highly intelligent if somewhat ditsy mother and say, The boy's talking sense, Rachel, and if that's the kind of wedding they want, that's the kind of wedding they should have. Anna smiled, then narrowed her eyes into a squint and peered at Baumgartner as if he were a stranger. Tell me, she said, how did you get to be such a conniving, duplicitous piece of work, Herr Baumgartner? Instead of answering her, Herr Baumgartner kissed his bride-to-be on the lips and said, One last thing, Anna. Not a single word about what happened to you on Claremont Avenue last night, agreed? Agreed, she said. Not today, not tomorrow, not one word ever.

That was the only money they ever took from Anna's parents, but their wedding gift of ten thousand dollars was such a colossal sum back then that they could look up at the sky now and no longer have to worry about when it was going to fall on top of them. They found a snug, two-and-a-half-bedroom apartment on Barrow Street in the West Village, and the next fall, when Baumgartner landed an assistant professorship in the philosophy department at the New School, they could both walk to their jobs. For the next twelve years, nothing changed. They went on living in their Barrow Street refuge, Anna went on working at Heller Books, where she rose from junior to senior editor and started translating as well, and Baumgartner went on teaching at the New School, where he moved on from assistant to associate to full professor and wrote his books on the phenomenology of reading and the politics of fear, every word composed in his little half-room at the back of the apartment, down the hall from the other little room where Anna wrote her poems, edited her authors, and translated her books. The point being this: it was the early golden age of their life together, and none of it would have happened in the way it did if the stubborn, idealistic Anna hadn't given some ground in order to turn the war she had been fighting for herself into a war for the two of them and accepted that money from her parents.

With Judith, everything was the same but reversed. A well-heeled Jewish family from the New York suburbs (Westport, Connecticut), an ambitious, hardworking father with a corporate law practice in Manhattan, a book-reading mother who did not work, and a childhood with a younger brother and sister that was filled with the same sorts of advantages Anna had received, but unlike the embattled Anna, the young Judith embraced the good life she had been born into and did not question it. A cheerleader in high school of all things, class president in her junior year, top grades and a hundred friends, a winner girl who then skipped thirty miles up the road and went to Yale. In spite of their similar backgrounds, she and Anna have nothing or nearly nothing in common, and that *nothing* is what puzzles Baumgartner the most whenever he stops and asks himself how he could have fallen so hard for two such different women. The raw, direct, and spontaneous Anna, and now the poised and sophisticated Judith, the impressive, self-assured Judith, a significant someone in the film world who has served on the juries of all the major festivals and has published four books so far with a fifth on the way, whereas the exuberant but inward-looking Anna devoted her immense literary talents to translating the work of others and hiding the best of who she was by hiding her poems from the world.

Judith has read those poems and knows how good they are, and one night about nine months ago, not long after it finally dawned on Baumgartner how much Judith had come to mean to him, he began a playful, half-jesting conversation with her by spouting a wild, crackpot theory about how Anna had predicted his future romance with a woman named Feuer in one of her early poems, a poem written so long ago that Judith had been in the second or third grade at the time, but there it is, he said to her that night, as they sat side by side on the sofa in her living room, there it is and there it was, and then he went on to explain that every time he thinks of the name Feuer, which means *fire* in German, he also thinks of Anna's little poem "Lexicon," the one about the tiny flower that has no name, the burning dot of red that jumps out from the asphalt and traps her in its spell, and because Anna's name was Blume, which means *flower* in German, he imagines that by some strange, alchemical process, the flower that turns into a flame is in fact Blume turning into Feuer, the passing of the torch from Anna to Judith, and there he is at the end of the poem, Herr Baumgartner himself, in the guise of the tiny imp grinning at Anna from across the street, with the flower-fire ablaze in his buttonhole, grinning because he's happy and wants to thank her for the present she's given him, which is you, dear Judith, Baumgartner said, my bright, burning fire-woman, *gleaming like a lit match in the dark.*

It was his way of telling Judith that she now stood shoulder to shoulder with Anna in his mind, and when Judith took hold of his hand, raised it to her mouth, and kissed it, Baumgartner felt certain that she understood what he had been trying to do. It was still too early to risk everything with an open declaration of love, and so he had resorted to this roundabout exercise in nutso literary analysis as a first step toward the moment when he would at last find the courage to bare his soul to her. After that night,

93

they went on as before, seeing each other two or three times a week, cooking dinner at his house or her house followed by a movie or else no movie as they went on talking about their work or Judith's kids or the deranged Ubu in the White House or told stories about their pasts and then bedded down together until morning. The same routine, but Baumgartner sensed that they were drawing closer now and that whatever invisible barriers had stood between them (caution? self-doubt? fear?) were gradually coming down. Then Baumgartner dreamed the dream and went off with Anna on their long walk through the memory palace, and once he returned, his caution, self-doubt, and fear slowly melted away. The *nothing in common* still confounds him, but instead of interpreting it as yet another sign of his flawed and incoherent approach to life, he now sees that *nothing* as a positive force. Judith is not Anna, and if and when he can persuade her to marry him, the life he leads with her will not be a continuation of his life with Anna but something altogether different and new, and how could anyone who has lived as long as he has ask for more than that? A chance to begin again. A chance to take chances again and ride through the whirlwind of whatever good or bad thing will be happening next.

It is Saturday, August 11, 2018. At seven o'clock in the evening, Baumgartner sets out on the four-block walk from his house to Judith's, carrying twelve red roses in the crook of his right arm and clutching the thornless stems firmly in his left hand as he ponders where and at what moment he should pop the question tonight. Sooner rather than later, he thinks, since putting it off would only increase his nervousness as the minutes ticked by, and if early is the best way to go about it, then why not spring into action at once? The scene begins to play out in his head, which he imagines will unfold more or less as follows: He will hand her the flowers the moment she opens the door, the smiling Judith will thank him with a tender buss on the cheek, and then the two of them will head for the kitchen to unwrap the flowers and search for a vase big enough to put them in, and because the kitchen is such a cozy, intimate place, no doubt the best place in the house for asking difficult, life-altering questions, he will fill the vase with water as Judith clips off the bottoms of the stems, and once he hoists the water-laden vase out of the sink, he will carry it over to her and set it down on the countertop, where Judith will put the roses in the vase and fuss with them for a while, arranging and rearranging them until the job is finished, at which point he will come up to her from behind, wrap his arms around her waist, lean forward until his mouth is brushing against her neck, and say, in his softest, most confiding voice: *I've been thinking* . . .

It is the end of another hot afternoon in central New Jersey, the land of cranberry bogs, swarming mosquitoes, and long, humid summers. As he expected he would when he shut the door of his house, Baumgartner is already sweating into his shirt by the time he comes to Judith's road. It will

95

be another hour before the sun goes down, but the sky is beginning to show the first faint signs of encroaching dusk and darkness, with touches of pink and orange now creeping along the edges of the clouds and a flock of swallows swooping in the distance, small visual wonders to compensate for the hours of sweat and sticky skin. By now, Baumgartner is walking down Judith's block with only six houses to go. He feels his lungs tighten, his stomach begins to clench, but even as the jitters spread through his body, he forces himself to quicken his pace, knowing that he must see this thing through to the end, even if it winds up killing him. He turns left onto the front walk of Judith's house, pauses for a moment to readjust the flowers in his arms, pauses for another moment to replenish the air in his lungs, and a moment after that he is ringing the bell.

For the first little while, everything goes as he imagined it would, but after the flowers have been fussed with and arranged and he comes up from behind to put his arms around her, he does not begin by saying *I've been thinking* . . . but rather by asking a question: *Is this enough for you—or do you want more?* It is an obscure, clumsily worded sentence, and Judith has trouble understanding it. What does he mean by *this*, she asks, and what is the thing she is supposed to want more of? Such an odd question, she says, since she is perfectly happy to be just where she is at this moment, standing in the kitchen with his arms wrapped around her body and his mouth nuzzling against her neck, and how could she ask for more of something that is already more than enough? Baumgartner apologizes for not making himself clear. He isn't talking about this moment, he says, which couldn't be better or more perfect than it is, but because (*kissing her neck*) he feels exactly as she does and because (*kissing her neck again*) what they have made together in the past couple of years is so deep and so good, he asked that dumbbell question of his to find out whether she wanted to stand pat or make some changes (*running his hands over her breasts as he kisses her neck again*), for the truth is, he says, that two or three times a week is no longer enough for him and he wants them to start spending more time together, as much time as possible, and he wonders if that same thought has ever occurred to her, and if it hasn't, whether she is for the idea or against it?

Ah, Judith says, now she understands. A hundred little tops are spinning around in that large, mighty brain of his, and he wants them to sit down and talk, doesn't he? Freeing her left arm from his grasp, she gestures to the kitchen table as Baumgartner drops both arms to his sides and Judith pads over to the refrigerator in her elegant Chinese slippers to fetch a cold bottle of wine. Meanwhile, Baumgartner is pulling out two glasses from a cupboard above the countertop and extracting a corkscrew from a drawer just below it, and by the time he puts them on the table, Judith is putting the bottle down beside them. They both pull out chairs and sit down, face-to-face on opposite sides of the table, and the big moment is suddenly upon him.

Baumgartner opens the wine and pours out two glasses. They each raise their glass to the other, each one takes a sip, and after they lower their glasses and put them on the table again, Judith begins.

They've come to a glorious place together, she says, and she feels happier with him than any man she has ever known. That much is certain. She loves him, and even if he has never said it in so many words, she knows that he loves her, and now that she has begun to have a more nuanced feel for how his mind works, she understands that the business about spending more time together is his way of building up to the much bigger question he is planning to ask her within the next three or four minutes.

You see right through me, don't you? Baumgartner says.

Not really. It's just that I've had that same thought myself about six hundred times in the past two months.

And what have you decided?

I've decided that I'm thrilled whenever I think about it. I've decided that I'm scared whenever I think about it. I've decided that I need more time to decide, and for now I want to go on in the same way we've been going and let the future decide the rest.

As her last words settle into him, Baumgartner begins to go numb. His head feels strange, as if his skull is suddenly expanding and filling up with emptiness, more and more emptiness until he is dazed and dizzy and drifting far, far away. Like a boxer, he thinks, like a mismatched boxer fighting out of his weight class, he has been flattened by a left hook, but Baumgartner is still conscious, still not down for the count, and as he slowly rises from the canvas on his wobbly legs, he manages to say this: Before we started sleeping together, I'd been living alone for eight years without feeling too lonely, muddling along in what I'd call a bearable sort of anguished isolation, but the moment you walked into my life, my life turned into a different life, and now I've come to hate living alone. After we spend a night together at my house, you leave in the morning and I'm stranded in the emptiness of all those rooms, wishing you were still there with me, and when we spend a night together here, I'm the one who has to leave in the morning and go back to that empty, haunted house. Loneliness kills, Judith, and chunk by chunk it eats up every part of you until your whole body is devoured. A person has no life without being connected to others, and if you're lucky enough to be deeply connected to another person, so connected that the other person is as important to you as you are to yourself, then life becomes more than possible, it becomes good. What we have is good, but it isn't good enough anymore, not for me, in any case, and the thing I don't understand is why the thought of marrying me should scare you off.

He sees the look of fierce concentration in Judith's eyes, he watches her assemble her thoughts, and then, ever so gently, she says: Our situations are completely different, Sy. You lost Anna after a long, beautiful marriage, and you were crushed by it for years. I got out of a long, brutal marriage to a man I came to despise, and I rejoiced when he packed his bags and left. That was only four years ago, and since then I've been a free woman, still responsible for my job, of course, but otherwise my own boss, in absolute control of every decision I make. That's why I'm in New York so often—because I want to be there. I'm invited to all kinds of things, and if there's a conference or a screening or a premiere I want to go to, I go. I enjoy all that bustling around, it invigorates me, and then I come back to Princeton to teach my classes and to be with you, the man I love, the man I want to go on loving for as long as he'll put up with me, which I hope is forever, and how could I want more than that? It's the life I've always dreamed of, Sy, and now I'm in the thick of it, living it out as fully as I can.

The conversation goes on for an hour and a half, but twenty or thirty minutes into it they are already beginning to repeat themselves, traveling back and forth over the same ground with only the slightest variations in their approach to the problem, for in spite of their contrasting positions on what to do next, each one understands the other's point of view and can even sympathize with it, but much as Baumgartner supports Judith's craving for freedom, autonomy, and self-fulfillment, he tells her, it makes no sense to him that she should think those things would be taken from her if they moved in together, which leads to the delicate subject of their first marriages and how he and Anna had both found freedom and self-fulfillment while living together in the same house, whereas Judith had felt increasingly smothered by the bitter, bombastic Joe, which explains why she is hesitating to take the plunge, she says, and he's bouncing up and down on the diving board, itching to jump in. She needs time, she says, and he mustn't pressure her into making a decision when she isn't ready, which is a good point, Baumgartner realizes, almost a warning, and therefore he backs off rather than pursue his line of argument, keeping his mouth shut just when he is about to tell her that none of this has anything to do with Anna or Joe and that the reason why this matter is more urgent for him than it is for her is that she has more time than he does, and depending on her interpretation of the word *time*, there's a good chance that he'll be dead before she ever gets around to making a decision. Nevertheless, this strategic withdrawal into silence begins to lower the temperature in the room, and before long she is granting him a small but important concession. One of the difficulties about their current arrangement is that the *two or three days a week* is too vague, he says. Tuesdays and Thursdays have been more or less fixed as the *two*, but the third day has been a constant source of trouble, again and again leading to an anxious scramble of phone calls and texts to pin down whether it is on or off, and if it is on, there is a further scramble to establish the when and the where and the how of it, and if it is off, he inevitably winds up feeling disgusted with himself for having put so much useless effort into a thing that turns out to be nothing more than a fat, fizzled-out nothingburger. I won't dispute that you need more time to answer the big question, he says, but on this much smaller question, I think we'll both be better off if we say yes to the third day, which usually seems to fall on a Saturday, so let's make it Saturday, come hell or high water, and if it happens to be a Saturday when you want to go to New York, I'll go with you and attend any conference or screening or premiere you're planning to go to, and then we'll spend the night in a swank hotel and order in a room service brunch on Sunday morning. Unless you've got some Johnny Hot-Pants stashed away in a secret hole on Second Avenue, of course, in which case I won't insist.

Judith seizes up with laughter at Baumgartner's lame imitation of a movie tough. Don't crack wise with me, mister, she says. I got one Johnny in my life, got it? And his initials are the same as yours, got it? So shut your trap and kiss me.

And so the conversation ends. Judith has turned him down, but at the same time she has offered him a little crumb, which is supposed to make him feel grateful, which he supposes he is, and yet, after settling for so little after hoping for so much, he understands that he has been reduced to the status of a mendicant, knocking on the back door of the palace and begging the royal scullery maid for some leftover scraps from the queen's plate.

When he walks home the following afternoon, which is four days before the tenth anniversary of Anna's death, he knows that he will be married only once in his life. Judith will keep putting him off until he gives up and walks away or else stays put and agrees to go on playing by her rules until the day comes when she walks away from him. He is too old for her, and she will never marry him, even though she does love him in her way, perhaps as much as he loves her, but he is only a pause in her life as she recovers from the wounds inflicted by her years with Joe, and once she is fully back on her feet she will fall into the arms of someone younger and more exciting than he is and that will be that.

Because all this comes to pass within the next nine months, and because Judith not only leaves Baumgartner for another man but also leaves New Jersey and heads out to California to accept a chair in the UCLA film department, we will dispense with a detailed account of those months. Instead, we will end the chapter with Baumgartner sitting at his desk, pen in hand, one hour after he has returned from Judith's house on August 12, 2018. He is scratching out another one of the many short fables he has written over the years, inconsequential nothings that he tosses into a drawer and has never bothered to show anyone, not even Anna. Still, he goes on writing them at moments of extreme duress, and with Baumgartner's spirits at a low ebb that afternoon as he mourns the death of what he feels has been his last chance at love, perhaps this odd confabulation will help the reader understand our hero's state of mind at that particular moment on that particular day.

LIFE SENTENCE

I had barely turned seventeen when the presiding judge of the Northern District handed down his verdict and sentenced me to what he called *a life of making sentences.* That was more than half a century ago, and since then I have lived alone in a cell on the third floor of Correctional Facility No. 7. I admit that the punishment was harsh, but to give the authorities their due, the door of my cell has never been locked, and there is little doubt in my mind that I could have walked out of here anytime I wanted. It's not that I haven't been tempted, but for reasons I have never fully understood, I have chosen to remain.

My jailer, who is an old man now, at least as old as I am if not older, has never spoken a word to me. For fifty-plus years, he has delivered my meals three times a day, and three times a day for the first twenty years he would laugh whenever he walked in and saw me hunched over the table working on my sentences. For the next twenty years, he would hold his hand against his mouth and snicker. Now he merely shakes his head and sighs.

There used to be another prisoner in the cell two doors down from mine, a man named Bronson or Brownson, and sometimes we would talk to each other about the bad food and the thin blankets on our beds, but Bronson or Brownson has said nothing to me for the past five or six years, which probably means he is dead. No doubt they carried him away one night while I was asleep.

From the silence in the corridor these days, I suspect that I am the last person in the solitary-confinement wing of the prison. It sounds lonely, I suppose, but it's not as bad as all that. Great effort is required to make a sentence, and great effort requires great concentration, and as one sentence must inevitably follow another in order to build a work composed of sentences, great concentration is required throughout the day, which means that the days pass by quickly for me, as if each hour that registers on the clock were no longer than a minute. After fifty-plus years of quickly passing days, it feels as if my life has rushed by in a blur. I have become old, but because the days have passed so quickly, most of me still feels young, and as long as I can still hold a pencil in my hand and still see the sentence in front of me, I suppose I will carry on with the same routine I have been following since the morning I arrived here. And if a moment should finally come when I can no longer carry on, all I have to do is get up and leave. If I am too old to walk by then, I will ask my jailer to help me. I am sure he will be glad to see me go.

4

One year and one month later, Baumgartner is sitting at the same desk in the same room puzzling over whether to keep the sentence he has just written or to cross it out and start again. He crosses it out, but before he starts again he lifts himself out of the chair, walks over to the open window, and looks down into the backyard. It is a splendid, sun-filled afternoon in mid-September, one of those brash, bullying days that storm into the house, grab you by the collar, and kick you outdoors, so rather than go back to his desk and struggle with the sentence for the third or fourth time, Baumgartner succumbs to the lure of the weather and leaves the room to head for the backyard, where he settles into a lawn chair midway between the back patio and the dogwood tree. He pats the left front pocket of his shirt and discovers that it is empty. No sunglasses. He must have left them in the bedroom yesterday, but even though the light is exceptionally brilliant this afternoon, he has no desire to traipse back into the house to search for them. On a day like this one, he says to himself, better to let the sun do its work of illuminating the world and to take it all in with naked, unprotected eyes.

He looks up, squinting into the air as a bird passes overhead. Such white clouds, he says to himself. Such pure white clouds pasted against all that blue, which has to be the bluest blue sky he has seen in years. Remarkable, he thinks. The earth is on fire, the world is burning up, yet for the time being there are still days like this one, and he might as well enjoy it while he can. Who knows if this isn't the last good day he will ever see—or the last day of any kind, for that matter? Not that he is expecting to drop dead before the birds wake up tomorrow morning, but facts are facts, and the numbers don't lie. He is seventy-one now, with yet another birthday looming in just six weeks, and once you enter that zone of diminishing returns, all bets are off.

Baumgartner looks down, intending to study the grass at his feet, but as his eyes travel southward, their journey is interrupted by the sight of the little paunch bulging from his once flat belly and the zipper of his pants, which is not zipped up as he thought it was but open, wide open. Baumgartner is aghast. Not again! he cries out to himself. Keep this up, nitwit, and it won't be long before you've forgotten your name.

Some time ago, when he was still in his forties and early fifties, he began to notice that many of his older friends and colleagues were forgetting to zip up after a visit to the men's room, the white-haired ones in their mid-seventies and early eighties who would wander back to their seats at restaurant tables unaware of the gaping barn doors just below their belts. At first, Baumgartner was amused by these harmless lapses. Then he felt both amused and saddened by them. Then saddened and not at all amused, for he had seen enough of them by that point to understand that the open fly is the beginning of the end, the first step on your way down the long hill to the bottom of the world. Now that it has started happening to him—*four times in the past two weeks*—he wonders how many months or years it will take before he becomes a full-fledged member of the club.

Nothing to be done, he thinks, nothing at all. Short-term memory loss is an inevitable part of growing old, and if it's not forgetting to zip your zipper, it's marching off to search the house for your reading glasses while you're holding the glasses in your hand, or going downstairs to accomplish two small tasks, to retrieve a book from the living room and to pour yourself a glass of juice in the kitchen, and then returning to the second floor with the book but not the juice, or the juice but not the book, or else neither one because some third thing has distracted you on the ground floor and you've gone back upstairs empty-handed, having forgotten why you went down there in the first place. It's not that he didn't do those kinds of things when he was young, or forget the name of this actress or that writer or blank out the name of the secretary of commerce, but the older you become, the more often these things happen to you, and if they begin to happen so often that you barely know where you are anymore and can no longer keep track of yourself in the present, you're gone, still alive but gone. They used to call it senility. Now the term is dementia, but one way or the other, Baumgartner knows that even if he winds up there in the end, he still has a long way to go. He can still think, and because he can think, he can still write, and while it takes a little longer for him to finish his sentences now, the results are more or less the same. Good. Good that *Mysteries of the Wheel* is coming along, and good that he has stopped work early today and is sitting out in the backyard on this magnificent afternoon, letting his thoughts drift wherever they want to go, and with all this circling around the business of short-term memory, he is beginning to think about long-term memory as well, and with that word *long*, images from the distant past start flickering in a remote corner of his mind, and suddenly he feels an urge to start foraging around in the thickets and underbrush of that place to see what he might discover there. So rather than go on looking at the white clouds and the blue sky and the green grass, Baumgartner shuts his eyes, leans back in his chair, tilts his face toward the sun, and tells himself to relax. The world is a red flame burning on the surface of his eyelids. He goes on breathing in and out, in and out, inhaling the air through his nostrils and exhaling through his partially opened lips, and then, after twenty or thirty seconds, he tells himself to remember.

The first thing that comes back to him is the family trip to Washington in the spring of 1956, the one time his frazzled, overworked parents ever pulled it together long enough to organize a journey beyond the outskirts of Newark, the first time the four Baumgartners would be sleeping in a place other than the apartment on Lyons Avenue, located directly above his parents' business, Trocadero Fashions, the marginally profitable dress shop that served the needs of the middle-class and lower-middle-class women of the neighborhood. Baumgartner was eight and a half, and little Naomi was not yet five. At seven o'clock on Friday morning, which was the one day in his childhood when Baumgartner was allowed to cut school, his father hung a sign on the front door of Trocadero Fashions that read: BACK ON MONDAY. Then the four of them piled into the family car, a dented blue Chevy that had rolled off the Clunkersville assembly line in 1950, and off they went to the nation's capital on a brilliant morning of white clouds and blue sky that turned into an afternoon eerily similar to this one, which is perhaps why Baumgartner is remembering the story now. Once they arrived, they checked into their hotel (name forgotten except for the *The* before the name), which was the first hotel he and his sister had ever set foot in, and, according to his mother, the first hotel she and his father had gone to since their honeymoon in the Catskills thirteen years earlier. For

Naomi, whose head was filled at the time with tales of fairy princesses, wicked sorcerers, and heroic young suitors in tights and velvet hats, the hotel was so large and so glorious that it had to be and most certainly was an enchanted castle, even if to Baumgartner's less clouded eyes, the place looked rather shabby and run-down, with fraying carpets and water stains on the bathroom ceiling.

It was a little past two by then. A slight pause while he and his parents unpacked their bags and Naomi ran back and forth between the adjoining rooms and dive-bombed onto the beds, and then they went out to explore the sights in that perfect May weather, the Capitol dome, the White House, the Supreme Court building, the cherry trees in bloom, the Mall, the obelisk, and the sainted one in his immense marble chair, but as the four of them walked through the streets of the city, his sister was growing agitated, more and more disturbed about something until at last she burst into tears. I want to go to Washington! she yelled. But you *are* in Washington, Baumgartner and his parents said to her. Look around you. Everything you see is Washington. No, she insisted, as tears streamed down her face, not *this* Washington—the real Washington! No one understood what she was talking about. For want of any other way to comfort her, Baumgartner's father picked her up and carried her in his arms so the walk could continue. Within two minutes, she fell asleep, and when they returned to the hotel half an hour later, his sister woke up just seconds after they walked through the door. She looked around the lobby and smiled. That's better, she said. Now we're back in the real Washington.

How she had adored him when they were young, the big brother who watched over her and reasoned with her and comforted her during the soul-shaking mood-storms that periodically jolted her off course, who entertained her with stories about the invisible people who lived on his left shoulder and caused no end of mischief to the evildoers who camped out on his right shoulder, the all-powerful Sy who could concoct such marvels and shield her against the blows of the universe, how she had looked up to him back then, and how, little by little, he had abandoned her as he emerged from his own childhood and stumbled into adolescence, slowly coming to the bleak conclusion that home was not a good place for him, that he detested the cramped, ugly apartment and the miserable dress shop downstairs, and therefore he drifted away from them and attached himself to the world of his friends, which before long became the big world beyond Newark, for lucky Sy was such a nimble student that they let him skip a grade when he was twelve and then, because his birthday fell in November, he graduated from Weequahic High School when he was just sixteen and was gone, off to the distant flatlands of rural Ohio on a four-year scholarship to Oberlin—which he buzzed through in three and a half—leaving the twelve-year-old Naomi to fend for herself in the dismal apartment above the dress shop, and so it was that the benevolent prince of her early childhood was transformed into a heartless, reprehensible toad. Or a turd. Or a toad in the shape of a turd.

He doesn't blame her for resenting him, but he was too young and too wrapped up in his own life to feel responsible for the fragile, tempestuous little creature who happened to have the same parents he did and at age three was given his bedroom, which forced him to spend his nights sleeping on the fold-out couch in the living room and to do his home-work at the school library or at Dickie Birnbaum's house down the block. There had been no one to watch over him when he was her age, after all, and he figured she would be able to handle things on her own as well. He was partly right and partly wrong. Right in the sense that she grew up into your average, high-strung neurotic and not a raving mad-woman, right in the sense that she was intelligent enough to go to college and pretty enough to attract the desires of various young men, one of whom she eventually married, but wrong in the sense that she could ever let go of her animos-ity toward him, Mr. Hotshot with his scholarship and his undergraduate year in Paris, Sir Know-It-All who flunked his draft board physical because of a falsely diagnosed heart murmur and promptly lit out for parts unknown, bounc-ing around the country and working odd jobs for the next seven months—carpenter's assistant in Missoula, moving man in Saint Paul, dishwasher in Chicago, housepainter in Charleston—with no sign of him except for an occasional postcard, and then graduate school at Columbia with yet another year in Paris and his dissertation on Merleau What's-His-Name, as if anyone gave a rat's ass about a dead French philosopher, and then his cushy job as an assistant professor at the New School, whereas she, the second-rate little sister, a graduate of Montclair State Teachers College and a schoolmarm to eleven- and twelve-year-old kids, was *down in the trenches of real life*, not strutting around with her head in the clouds and posing as a goddamned *intellectual*. Again and again, Baumgartner would say to her: Contrary to what you might think, Naomi, I happen to share your opinion. Without you, there would be no future. Without me, the future would take care of itself. There's no comparison. We're both teachers, yes, but your job is far more important than mine. To which Naomi would respond: Ha!

Baumgartner breaks off in mid-thought and asks himself what the hell he is doing. Why go back and beat that dead horse when he is supposed to be crawling around in the woods with a hand rake and a toy shovel digging up little treasures from the Neolithic past, the sting in his nose and the burn in his throat when he sneaked his first shot of whiskey at twelve, for example, or the mysterious warmth that spread through his body as he experienced his first adolescent hard-on, or, at fifteen, the tearful, pulverizing effect of listening to the *Saint Matthew Passion* for the first time. Or, pushing it in a slightly different direction, to relive moments of walking through waist-high snowdrifts as a little boy or climbing trees as a bigger boy or punching back after being punched by a Jew-baiting moron in a black motorcycle jacket as an even bigger boy, or, perhaps more pertinently, to investigate why some fleeting, random moments persist in memory while other, supposedly more important moments vanish forever. His high school graduation is completely gone now, for example, the color of his first bicycle has been erased, and there is nothing left of any one of the students who came to his early morning class on the pre-Socratics three times a week during his first semester at the New School, not one name, not one face, but he remembers the little girl on the train half a century ago and has thought about her hundreds of times since then. Why that girl, a person he never even spoke to, and not one of those fourteen or fifteen students?

It was the end of his time on the road, the rugged months of silence, physical work, and relentless self-examination, late summer 1968, the apocalyptic year of fire and blood, the year of America's collective nervous breakdown, and there he was traveling from Charleston to New York on a low-budget milk train that took twenty-four hours from start to finish with stops at every jerkwater town along the way. Six or seven stops into the ride, the little girl boarded the train with her mother, both of them dressed as Baumgartner imagined they would have dressed for church on Sunday, a black church in this case, as the girl and her mother were black, two black Southerners at a time when Jim Crow was still breathing even though it had been pronounced legally dead, and to step onto an integrated train and ride it for many hours under the scrutinizing gaze of white people demanded that you look your best and comport yourself with utmost dignity and composure. They took their seats two rows in front of Baumgartner on the other side of the aisle, and because the mother and her daughter were facing south and Baumgartner was facing north, he had a clear, unobstructed view of them for the full length of their journey, which, if he is not mistaken, ended in Washington nine or ten hours later. He can't remember if they had packed any food or whether they paused to eat along the way, but what he does remember is that the little girl was wearing white gloves, as perfectly white as the white clouds drifting overhead this afternoon, pristine white gloves, a starched and ironed party frock, the color now forgotten, white anklets, and a pair of black, mirror-smooth Mary Janes on her feet, an impressively decked out little person, proof of the meticulous care this child received from her mother, but even more impressive to Baumgartner was the self-control the little one maintained throughout the long ride, sitting stock-still with her hands folded on her lap for all those hours, shoulders back, spine straight, an exquisitely erect posture, occasionally turning her head to look out the window, occasionally whispering something into her mother's ear, occasionally listening to her mother whisper something into her ear and nodding or shaking her head or smiling in response. She had no doll

117

with her, no book, no toy to distract her from the tedium of the slowly moving train, which meant that she did nothing but sit there and look into the middle distance in front of her, either thinking or dreaming or musing in the same way Baumgartner has always thought and dreamt and mused, never fidgeting as Naomi would have done at that age, never whining or complaining as Naomi had continued to when she was twice the girl's age, and as Baumgartner went on studying this exceptional child, he asked himself if she was acting out of pride or fear or a combination of the two. No doubt her mother had instructed her on how she was supposed to behave during the trip, but it was impossible to know if those instructions had also come with a threat of harsh consequences if she failed to perform as expected, a thrashing, perhaps, or some other dreaded form of punishment, or, more likely, Baumgartner felt, since the mother struck him as a kind mother, a woman on her guard because of the circumstances but nevertheless a kind mother who was training her daughter how to exist in the American present as much by example as by word, and because the girl idolized her mother and wanted to emulate her in all things, she did what she was told without questioning, but also without fear. Eventually, the little girl leaned her head against her mother's shoulder, closed her eyes, and fell asleep. The mother put her arm around her daughter, looked down at her for a while, and then turned her head toward the window and studied the passing scenery all the way to Washington.

Two years later, there was another child on another train, this one a ten- or eleven-year-old boy, and this time the train was underground, the Paris Métro charging through a tunnel on its way from where to where he can no longer recall, nor the time of year, nor the time of day, although he suspects it was early evening, since the car was fairly crowded and growing more crowded after each new stop, with Baumgartner planted on one of the benches and numerous other passengers on their feet, clinging to poles and overhead straps, a noisy old Métro car with metallic wheels screeching along the iron rails and the lovely doors of varnished wood with the silver handles that had to be pushed up by the knob for the doors to spring open. He can still see those things, still feel those things—indelible flotsam from the unvanished but long vanished past. He must have glanced up from the book or newspaper he was reading, for at some point he discovered that he was looking at the boy and his father, who were standing directly in front of him at one of the poles, face-to-face with each other, for the most part standing in silence, although every now and then one would lean forward and say something to the other, but the wheels of the train were too loud for Baumgartner to make out a word they said. The ten- or eleven-year-old was a good-looking, medium-sized boy, neither scrawny nor plump, neither dark nor fair, a work in progress who appeared to be a thoughtful, well-behaved kid on an outing with his father, and from the look in the boy's eyes, Baumgartner thought he detected a hint of quiet satisfaction, which suggested that solo outings with his father were rare events. As for the father himself, he seemed to be little more than a lump of human flesh, a soft-bellied, gray-faced man who could have been a minor functionary or a bank clerk or an office worker of some kind, a dreary sort who couldn't have been much beyond his late thirties or early forties but had already been ground down by his job or his life or the world and had no hope of ever getting back on his feet. Or so Baumgartner imagined, even as he told himself he was probably wrong. For all he knew, the bright, promising boy could have been a petty thief and future stick-up man, and the weary father could have been a paragon of strength and inner fortitude. Then, in the midst of these jumbled speculations, which are still alive in Baumgartner to this day, the boy leaned forward and said something to his father, and a moment after that the father hauled off and slapped the boy across the face. A hard, violent slap for no discernible reason—as loud as a pistol shot, as swift as a bullet fired into the boy's chest. For forty-nine years, Baumgartner has been pondering what the boy could have said to provoke such an extreme and humiliating response, and even though he knows he will never know, he goes on asking himself what it could have been. The boy was so stunned that for two or three seconds he just stood there, locked in place, and then he lifted his hand and pressed it against the assaulted cheek, which must have been stinging terribly by then, and a moment after that he lowered his head and looked down at the floor, his face crumpling up in misery, even as he struggled to push back the tears that were gathering in his eyes. The father looked on in his own private misery, horrified by what he had done, recoiling from the fury that had burst forth from his hand and driven him to attack his boy, as if, for the first time since he had become a father, he was beginning to understand that fathers have unlimited power over their sons, and to abuse that power is to turn yourself into a tyrant and a thug. Whatever the man might have been thinking, he couldn't bring himself to talk to his son, who was crying in earnest now and still hadn't looked up from the floor. Utterly at a loss, the father reached into his pocket and extracted a handkerchief, which he held out to the boy at a sufficiently low angle for the boy to see it, even though he refused to lift his eyes from the floor. He took the handkerchief and covered his face with it, but still he refused to look up. The father said nothing. Twenty seconds later, the train arrived at Baumgartner's stop. He rose from his seat, walked over to one of the doors, maneuvered the metal latch until the door slid open, and stepped out onto the platform. He turned around for a last look, but the boy and his father were blocked from sight by a crowd of new passengers boarding the train.

His father had never slapped him. Nor had he ever punched him or kicked him or even spanked him, but Baumgartner's father had been an old father, and who knows if he wouldn't have knocked him around from time to time if he had been younger and more vigorous. Born in Warsaw,

1905, dead in Newark, 1965. Not a long life by contemporary standards, but how can you expect to carry on into your dotage if you consume four packs of cigarettes a day and subsist on a diet composed largely of borscht, pickled herring, and hard-boiled eggs? Not lung cancer but a pulmonary embolism, which came down to the same thing but was quicker and more efficient: a massive clot travels up from your leg and invades your left lung, and one minute later you're a mote of cosmic dust.

For the second time in the past five minutes, Baumgartner stops in mid-thought and asks himself what he is doing. The last thing he wants is to spend the afternoon thinking about his family, and yet he started this little excursion into the past by remembering the family trip to Washington, which led to all that nonsense about his sister, and now he's on to his father as well. It's not that he hasn't tried to steer himself away from the subject, but even when he called up those two stories about the children on the trains and was thinking about the girl and her mother and the boy and his father, he was also thinking about himself and his parents, for it is clear to him now that those children have gone on haunting him for all these years because he saw them as stand-ins for himself as a child, and if there is no escape from the territory he has wandered into against his will, which in fact he has entered precisely according to his will, then Fuck it, Baumgartner says to himself, let's saddle up the old horse and ride it through to the end.

Tecumseh. That first of all and perhaps above all else, the middle name bestowed on him by his splenetic, contrarian father that allowed Baumgartner to forgo the dreadful *Seymour* and sign his books and conduct his professional life under the name of S.T. Baumgartner. It was nothing if not an unorthodox name for a white American family to give to a son born in the middle of the twentieth century, let alone to a Jewish-American son from Newark by way of Poland and points east of Poland, but it turned out that his self-taught, prodigiously well-read father, who called himself an *anarcho-pacifist* and *godless militant*, had ranked the Shawnee chief above all other Americans who had ever lived and had conferred the name Tecumseh on his son as a badge of honor. In the days after his father's death, when Baumgartner was still just seventeen, he found a thick, unstamped envelope among his father's things marked with the words: *To My Son On The First Day Of His Life.* The letter was supposed to have been handed over to him on his thirteenth birthday, but true to form, his father had filed it away somewhere and forgotten about it. Nevertheless, in his old man's most florid, overblown style, the last paragraph explained why Tecumseh stood out as such an important figure for him: . . . because he was a man of courage, humanity, and highest intelligence who sought to unite his disparate, far-flung people into resisting the European invaders who were out to destroy the Shawnee nation and every other Indian nation across the length and breadth of this doomed, blood-soaked continent. No matter that he had died in the struggle. Tecumseh fought the good fight. And that is all I will ever ask of you, my newborn son, in the first hours of your long journey toward becoming a man who can think and act and take part in the world—only this and nothing else: to fight the good fight.

Even then, fifty-four years ago, Baumgartner realized that his father had probably been drunk when he wrote those words, and as the aging son sorts through his conflicted memories of that father now, he finds himself turning his thoughts to the letter and trying to imagine the circumstances under which those three and a half pages had been written. A forty-two-year-old man has just become a father for the first time. He has left his young wife and newborn son at the hospital and has returned to the empty apartment above the dress shop on Lyons Avenue. He cuts off a slab of rye bread from the loaf on the kitchen counter, prepares a modest portion of herring for himself, and sits down at the table, where a shot glass and a bottle of slivovitz are already waiting for him. He eats and drinks, and after he has finished eating, he drinks two or three more shots. It is a solemn but exultant moment for him, an occasion unlike any other in his life, and this tough-minded, often hard-hearted man is engulfed by large waves of feeling, an oceanic surge rising from his gut and up through his throat that pulls him out of himself long enough for him to understand how small he is, a small thing connected to the trillions of other small things that compose the universe, and how good it feels to have left himself behind for now and to have become a part of the vast, floating enigma of life. Forty-two years old and at last a father, he thinks. Forty-two years of failure and frustration, and now this unlikely turn into something that resembles happiness, at least for this one night, at least for these few hours, and so he gathers up the bottle and the glass and goes off to the spare room at the other end of the apartment, the one that only he is allowed to enter and which would later be turned over to Baumgartner and eventually to Naomi, but on this particular night in November 1947, it is still his father's exclusive realm, an unadorned nine-by-twelve-foot enclosure with a desk and a chair in it along with several bookcases, shelf after shelf of ragged, mostly secondhand volumes of anarchist and socialist literature mixed in with dozens of books on European and American history. Newer books, all of them borrowed from the public library, lie in random heaps on the floor, many of them long past due. His father places the bottle and the glass on his desk, pours himself another shot, drinks it down, pulls out a small stack of blank paper from the top drawer to his left, uncaps his fountain pen, and begins his letter to Seymour Tecumseh Baumgartner on the first day of the boy's life. In it, he talks about his hopes of building a better world, a more just world, of living in a society of equals that would be run not by the laws of the jungle (capitalism) or the laws of the machine (Marxism) but by the natural laws of organic process and growth that would lead to a new social arrangement called *democratic communalism.* The language is inflated, the message is somewhat unclear, but the tone is gentle and persuasive, and when Baumgartner thinks of all the anger and cynicism that poured out of his father whenever he started in on one of his political rants over the years that followed, he sees the night of his birth as the one moment when his old man climbed down from his high horse and revealed the depth of the idealism that burned inside him. If nothing else, there is that, Baumgartner says to himself, as he looks up at the sky again and tracks the movement of a slowly passing cloud. At least there is that, and along with that there is Tecumseh, which evens the score for the first-name blunder and has made him S.T. to the world, Sy to his friends and beloveds, and Seymour to no one but a dead grade-school teacher from the distant, barely remembered past.

His father started out in life as Jakov the Pole but was reinvented as Jacob the Greenhorn when he landed here at age six, the third of five children born to Solomon and Ida Baumgartner, two girls before him and a pair of twin boys after, making him the oldest son, schooled from an early age in the delicate craft of needle-and-thread work by his father, a third-generation tailor who opened a shop on Newark's Market Street in 1912 and lived with the hope that one day he would pass on the business to his first-born son. According to the little Baumgartner had been told about his father's early life (mostly from his mother), young Jacob was an apt but reluctant pupil who had no interest in filling anyone's shoes but his own. Books were far more compelling to him than the drudgery of operating a sewing machine, and when he was eleven or twelve he abandoned his part-time after-school work for his father to concentrate on his studies, harboring intellectual aspirations that one day were going to free him from the trap of becoming a fourth-generation ragman, college for one thing, with an advanced degree in history to follow, or perhaps a course in the law to become a left-wing advocate of the poor and the downtrodden, or perhaps to bypass the law for a lawless life as an agitator and organizer of those same downtrodden workers—rent strikes, sit-ins at sweatshops, orchestrating marches and rallies in the streets of cities. Jacob started down that road with a number of small steps, constrained by financial circumstances from taking any of the large steps he had imagined earlier. Still, he felt he was moving in a positive direction, attending night school and holding down a day job at the Newark Public Library, but the financial constraints forced him to go on living at home, and with his two older sisters locked in dead-end marriages to slimy ne'er-do-wells, and his two younger brothers rapidly devolving into unemployable idiots, Jacob understood that he had to get out of there or drown, but for all his foresight about the living death that awaited him, he couldn't get out. His father's eyesight was weakening, his health was in decline, and when he was too far gone to carry on with the business, it was either sell the business and watch the family go to hell or keep the business breathing, so the twenty-two-year-old Jacob dropped out of night school, quit his job at the library, and took over the shop on Market Street. As it was told to Baumgartner, his father felt he had no choice. Of course he had a choice. Everyone has a choice, and the one his father made was not necessarily the wrong one, even though it embittered him for the rest of his life, but if he had made the opposite choice and run off to become a history professor or a lawyer or a footloose troublemaker, he probably would have tormented himself for the rest of his life over the unpardonable sin of having left his family in the lurch at its time of greatest need, which would suggest that there was no right choice or wrong choice, only two right choices that both would have come out wrong in the end. In Baumgartner's father's case, his sense of responsibility had won out over his desires for himself, which made his choice an honorable one, even a noble one, but if you begin to feel that your self-sacrifice has been wasted on a family of morons and mooching chiselers, your choice will inevitably turn into a source of resentment, and, as the years go on, inflict serious damage on your soul.

By the time Baumgartner came into the picture, the men's haberdashery store on Market Street had been replaced by the dress shop on Lyons Avenue. Solomon and Ida were long gone, the wayward twins had drifted out to California after serving time for a jewelry store heist in Weehawken, and Bella, the older of the two older sisters, had dumped her bookie husband and married a used car dealer from Perth Amboy, who was later dumped in his turn, which led to Bella's longtime employment as bookkeeper and manager of her brother's dress shop, while Emma, the younger of the two older sisters, gave birth to two daughters, was abandoned by her restless, out-of-work husband, and died of pneumonia in her mid-thirties, with Bella taking charge of the two orphaned girls and raising them on the salary she earned from her brother. In 1936, one year before he signed the mortgage on the Lyons Avenue building, Jacob had toyed with the idea of chucking it all and enlisting in the Abraham Lincoln Brigade to fight Franco and the fascists in the Spanish Civil War, but as he was morally opposed to the bearing of arms in any war, no matter how just, he didn't go through with it. A bad mistake, as he later told his son, letting down his guard after one too many drinks on a cold winter night when Baumgartner was a junior in high school, a bad mistake because he was already thirty-one by then, and after that there would be no more chances to *break free*. In mid-April 1939, the twenty-year-old Ruth Auster began working as a seamstress at Trocadero Fashions, and four years after that, in the middle of the Second World War, Baumgartner's parents were married.

The man who reigned over the Lyons Avenue household was a human conundrum of such daunting impenetrability that Baumgartner had spent his boyhood locked in a state of continual uncertainty about who his father was and who he was in relation to his father. He had feared and worshipped that father, at times he had almost loved him, but nothing about him had ever made any sense: an anti-capitalist capitalist who spent close to forty years running a small family business whose business was to make money for the family, a lowly man of the people and defender of the exploited masses who abused the people who worked for him with nasty insults and foul-tempered reprimands, an unrepentant atheist who forced his son to go through the ritual of a bar mitzvah because he himself had been forced to do that and wanted the boy to suffer as much as he had—but never mind that garbage now, Baumgartner says to himself, the essential thing was that for all his bluster and bombast and occasional bursts of cruelty, his father was little more than a hapless dreamer, a phantom revolutionary who sat in his room and never joined forces with any group of like-minded men and women or lifted a finger to take part in the smallest collective action to advance the cause of justice, a cut-off, isolated man who lived the struggle in his head and therefore lived with the knowledge that he had failed himself by not fighting what he imagined to be the *good fight*. It was all just talk in the end, but as the years rolled on no one from his diminishing circle of acquaintances would even talk to him anymore except his boyhood friend Milton Freyberg, a high school history teacher and ex-Communist who had quit the party over the Hitler-Stalin pact in '39 and lost his teaching job in the McCarthy purges of the early

fifties, a plump, burnt-out man who now made his living as
a researcher for Collier's Encyclopedia, meeting up for his
weekly dinners at Moishe's Restaurant with the burnt-out
noncombatant from the war against fascism, Baumgartner's
gaunt beanpole father, the Polish-American Quixote of sad
countenance and book-addled brain, king of the *luftmenschen*
who ran his little dress shop on Lyons Avenue by letting his
wife and sister do the work while he holed up in the second-
floor bedroom reading Emma Goldman's autobiography for
the seventh time. Drink up, old friend, Freyberg would say
to him, and have another schnapps while I have one myself.
Then we'll roll up our sleeves and duke it out for the seven
hundred and fourteenth time and see if one of us can save the
world before they turn off the lights and kick us out of here.

Still, there was one thing about his father, one important thing that Baumgartner began to sense when he was
ten or eleven and then knew for certain when he was twelve
and they let him skip the eighth grade. His father was proud
of him. Not that the old man ever said it, and not that he
didn't go out of his way to warn Baumgartner not to get a
swelled head each time he was presented with another one
of the boy's stellar report cards, reminding him that he was
made of dirt just like everyone else and would end up as dirt
just like everyone else no matter what his grades said, but in
spite of that grumpy posturing, Baumgartner knew that his
father was keeping a close eye on him, that Jacob the Crank
was reliving his own boyhood struggles through his son and

secretly urging him to break out of this mean little nowhere and fly away, fly as far away from home as his feeble wings could take him. Then, in March 1964, word came from distant Ohio about the scholarship that had fallen down on the unsuspecting Newark dirt-boy, and when Baumgartner handed his father the letter and told him to read it, he saw his father's hand shake—ever so slightly—and saw his eyes mist up—ever so briefly—and then his father took hold of the back of a kitchen chair, pulled it out from the table, sat down, discharged a long, shuddering exhale from his dam-aged lungs, and said: Fetch the bottle from the cupboard, Sy. It's time for a drink. Baumgartner returned with the bottle as his father lit his umpteenth Lucky of the day, and after the boy had lit one for himself, they each drank down a shot of slivovitz, but nothing more was said since everything had already been said in the letter, so they sat there drinking in silence, first one shot, then a second shot, and at last a third. His father's praise was in that silence. A man who ran at the mouth at the least provocation, a fulminating word-bag who could drone on for hours at a stretch, rewarded his son by keeping his mouth shut and saying nothing. Six months after that night, Baumgartner left for Ohio. He returned to Newark for Christmas break and went back to Ohio in January, not expecting to return again until the close of the second semester in June. Instead, he returned in February, February ninth to be exact, which was two days after his father's sixtieth birthday and one day after his father's death.

Baumgartner was shaken by that death but not undone by it. He wished he could have felt more, but the truth was that he couldn't, and all through that strange, unsettling week in Newark, with the shop closed and Aunt Bella boozing it up in the kitchen as she shouted curses at her dead baby brother while the thirteen-year-old Naomi hid in her room sobbing or shrieking at *fat, blubber-faced* Aunt Bella to shut up, Baumgartner was less concerned about himself or those two nutjobs than he was about his mother, the one point of sanity in an otherwise wholly demented household, Baumgartner's steadfast consoler and protector during his long march through childhood and a person who had grown up under much tougher circumstances than his father had, groomed for a life of no expectations as opposed to the high expectations his father had carried for himself and then failed to live up to, a young woman who had married when she was still in the process of discovering who she was and why she had been put on this earth, whereas her much older husband (by fourteen years) had nothing more to discover about himself except where he stood with her, his young bride, and the two children they would eventually make together.

As a boy, Baumgartner had known far less about her side of the family than his father's, the obscure Auster side that had no aunts or uncles or cousins in it, not one living relative anywhere in sight and hence no one to tell him anything about the family's history—only his mother, who knew almost nothing about it herself. All she had ever told him was that her father's name was Harry and that he had emigrated to America from a small Galician city in the easternmost part of the Austro-Hungarian Empire and that he had wound up in Brooklyn, where he married a woman whose name Baumgartner's mother had never known or else had forgotten, fathered three or four sons with her, whose names were also never known or forgotten, and then, sometime during the First World War, most likely in 1915 or 1916, his wife of the past seven or ten or twelve years sued him for divorce, settled for a onetime lump payment that cleaned out his bank account, and promptly left with the boys for Chicago, or Cleveland, or Cincinnati, or some other Midwestern city that began with a *C*, and was never heard from again. Harry moved to Manhattan, hustled up some money to go into business as a building contractor, did well enough to pay back the loan within a year, and in early 1918 married a woman named Millie Koplan. Thirteen months after the wedding, on March 7, 1919, Harry's second wife gave birth to Baumgartner's mother, Ruth, and just eighteen months after that the luckless Harry Auster fell off a scaffold hanging against the façade of a ten-story building near Washington Square and died when his body hit the sidewalk. Baumgartner's mother therefore had no memories of her father, and because Millie disappeared from her life when Ruth was not yet three, only the dimmest memories of her mother.

For most of his childhood, Baumgartner's mother protected him by refusing to explain what she meant by the word *disappeared.* He was too dumb back then to press her to be more specific and concluded that it must have been another word for death, one of those polite, evasive terms such as *passed* or *passed away* or *passed on* that allowed you to talk about death without having to say the word. Baumgartner was old enough to know that everyone dies and that even he himself was going to die one day, but he was still young enough to think that death comes only to the old, in most cases to the very, very old, and the confusing thing about his grandmother's death was that she hadn't been old, since his mother had said she was nineteen when she married his grandfather and twenty when she gave birth to her daughter, and if she had disappeared before his mother's third birthday, that meant she had died at twenty-two or twenty-three, which was a far cry from the customary sixty or seventy or eighty and suggested that some terrible thing had happened to her, some flukish accident such as being run over by a bus or falling off a scaffold or being shot down in the crossfire of a bank holdup—walking along the street one morning on her way to the butcher shop and then *bang*, she was dead, shot through the heart by a thirty-eight caliber slug.

It wasn't until he was fourteen that his mother finally opened up to him and told him the story. Yes, she said, it's true that her mother had disappeared, but contrary to what he had supposed, she hadn't died, she had simply married again, this time to a much older and wealthier man than poor Harry had ever been, a widower of fifty with three grown children from his first marriage who wanted no part in raising a fourth, so Millie and her new husband consulted a lawyer, papers were drawn up, and legal guardianship of little Ruthie was turned over to Harry's younger brother, Joseph, a semiliterate bachelor who worked as a repairman at a metalworks factory across the river in Newark. The contract included a cash payment of five or ten thousand dollars to help Joseph with the care of his niece (Baumgartner's mother never knew the exact amount), and a short time after that, Millie and her new husband left New York and moved to a far-off city thousands of miles away, where the husband set up a new branch of whatever business or enterprise he owned or directed. Either London or Los Angeles, Baumgartner's mother thought, in any case a city that began with the letter *L*, but that was all she remembered, since Uncle Joseph never talked to her about her mother, who by mid-1922 had well and truly *disappeared* and never saw her daughter again.

The fourteen-year-old Baumgartner was horrified when he heard this, both horrified and enraged by the magnitude of Millie's indifference, a mother tossing aside her little girl as if she were nothing more than a candy wrapper or a speck of lint marring the surface of her satin dress. Flick—and it's gone. What she had done was criminal, he said to himself, a crime against humanity, and just as Eichmann had been condemned to death last year for his crimes during the war, his odious grandmother Millie deserved to be hanged for hers. He couldn't bring himself to say these things out loud, however, since his mind was churning by then and he couldn't summon the words to express the horror that was growing inside him. All he managed to get out of his mouth was one sentence: She sold you down the river and split. And then, after a two- or three-second pause: How you must hate her.

No, his mother said, she didn't hate her, she pitied her, and before he judged her and started filling up with hate himself, he should try to imagine the kind of spot she was in. A young woman with nothing going for her except her beauty and power to attract men loses her husband in her early twenties and is left with a pile of unpaid bills and a small kid and no family to turn to for support. What are her options? She has to find a job, but if she goes to work, who will take care of the kid? She'll have to put her in an orphanage, or else not work and let the two of them starve to death, or else start walking the streets and sell her body to keep body and soul together, even if she loses her soul in the process. Then a rich man falls for her, falls so hard that rather than stash her away in an apartment and keep her as his mistress, he wants to marry her. She feels it's the one chance she'll ever have—a ticket out of hell and a one-way trip to a new and better life—and if she has to give up her daughter to have that life, she'll do it, not because she wants to do it but because she feels she has no choice. Rich or not, Baumgartner's mother said, that second husband must have been a crud—to force the woman he says he loves to make that kind of decision about her own child. If there's anyone to hate in this story, he's the one you should hate, Sy. It's not that she didn't do an awful thing to me, a selfish and disgraceful thing, but at least I can understand why she did it, and after thinking about it for all these years, I've come to realize that it was probably all for the best, because if that's the kind of mother she was, then maybe it's lucky that I didn't have to grow up with her. I got Uncle Joseph instead, the kindest, most gentle man on earth, as I've already told you a hundred times, so everything worked out in the end. I had a wonderful childhood, a full and happy childhood, and my mother played no part in it. She was like an actress who gets one scene in a movie, and then the scene is dropped because no one thinks it's any good. What's that expression they use? You know, when someone's in the movie and then isn't in the movie when you go to see it in the theater.

She died on the cutting-room floor.

That's it. She died on the cutting-room floor.

Baumgartner has no doubt that his mother was happy with her uncle and thrived under his care, since she never would have turned into the strong, steady person she became if she hadn't. Perhaps she tended to exaggerate a little when she told her stories about Uncle Joseph, and perhaps she tended to see her young self through a scrim of mythological wonderment as the cast-off waif in a Victorian melodrama who is rescued by the goodness of a simple, saintly man, but none of that matters now, for whatever real or imagined

paradise she lived in after the age of three came to an abrupt
end midway between her sixteenth and seventeenth birth-
days when fifty-four-year-old Joseph was struck down by
a gigantic, thunderbolt heart attack after working a double
shift at the metalworks factory. It was far and away the biggest loss of her life, immeasurably greater than her father's
death or her mother's disappearance, for the inescapable
fact was that she was entirely on her own now, a girl with
friends but no relatives, and no older person to turn to for
advice. Worst of all, there was no more Uncle Joseph, but
even in death he was still looking out for her and making
her transition into life without him as painless as possible.
For many years, he had been a staunch, dues-paying member of the Workmen's Circle, the old *Der Arbeter Ring*, the
mutual aid society set up by Yiddish-speaking immigrants
when he was a young man and newly arrived in America,
and because those dues provided burial assistance and low-
cost life insurance, Baumgartner's mother not only did not
have to pay for Joseph's funeral but received a check for
six thousand dollars from the life insurance policy—two
miracles in a black and hopeless world from the sublime and
munificent Workmen's Circle, which ran the after-school
programs in theater, music, and sewing she had attended
as a girl and sponsored Kinder Ring, the summer camp on
Sylvan Lake in Hopewell Junction that Uncle Joseph had
sent her to for four three-week stints in a row when she was
nine, ten, eleven, and twelve, which again and again she

had told the young Baumgartner were the most glorious summers of her life.

Even now, he still aches whenever he thinks about the crushing, unbearable loneliness that must have fallen on her during those miserable months in 1935. Just sixteen years old, an ordinary high school girl in the midst of living her life with only the vaguest notion of where she would be headed in the future, and then, from one day to the next, she was on her own and fully in charge of herself, an unprepared teenager suddenly forced into becoming an adult. She stayed on in the Shephard Avenue apartment surrounded by Uncle Joseph's things, but by the end of the year everything else about her life had changed. In high school, her best subjects had been math, science, music, art, and home economics, but she had always struggled in English, history, and French, not because she wasn't bright but because reading gave her trouble and she read too slowly to keep up with the work. As Baumgartner later discovered, she had been suffering from dyslexia since childhood, but no teacher had ever diagnosed the problem or done anything to help her, so she had fallen behind and began to think of herself as *stupid*, and with that word blaring in her head every morning when she walked into school, she shuffled through the halls with a sense of shame pressing down on her shoulders, and the pretty, fun-loving Ruth Auster became the shy and uncertain girl that no one knew quite what to make of anymore. Three months after Uncle Joseph's death, she dropped out of school, but not before she had a long talk with her sewing teacher, Mrs. Mancuso, who had once praised her in front of the class as the most gifted student she had ever had. The rotund, motherly Mrs. M. took hold of Ruth's hands and kept on holding them throughout the conversation. If she wanted to become a professional seamstress, she said, she could enroll in an intensive one-year course at a trade school or start working somewhere as an apprentice. Baumgartner's mother said she would prefer to skip school and go to work right away, but the problem was where. Mrs. Mancuso smiled and said, I don't think that will be a problem, dear.

After the two miracles from the Workmen's Circle, Mrs. Mancuso was the third miracle, and the fourth was her sister, Rosalie McFadden, the legendary dressmaker who ran Madame Rosalie's on Academy Street in downtown Newark, which to Baumgartner only proved, for the ten trillionth time in human history, that we are all dependent on one another and that no person, not even the most isolated person among us, can survive without the help of others. As in the case of Robinson Crusoe, who would have perished if Friday hadn't shown up to rescue him.

Three years later, on the strength of an emphatic telephone call from her boss to a man named Baumgartner, Ruth was hired to fill the open position of head seamstress at Trocadero Fashions. It wasn't that she wanted to change jobs, but the aging Madame Rosalie was calling it quits and retiring to Florida with her husband. As Baumgartner's mother liked to tell it, she had *recovered her bounce* as an employee in that shop, working her way up from lowly apprentice to trusted protégé, but now the shop was closing, and it was time to move on. In many ways, the new job would be a big step down from Madame Rosalie's fashionable, high-end business with its clientele of rich women from the suburbs, many of whom could afford to walk past the rows of pricey ready-to-wear stuff and head straight for the back room, where Madame Rosalie designed custom-made dresses for them and spectacular wedding gowns for their daughters, all of which were put together by her six-woman squad of seamstresses in the back-back room, where young Ruthie slowly and steadily emerged as the brightest light among them. There would be no more custom-made dresses at Trocadero, but the job seemed to be the best one available at the time. The salary was decent, and the shop was close enough to where she lived that she could walk to work, which meant no more standing on crowded rush-hour buses every morning and evening and no more bus fares nipping into her salary. In any case, she wouldn't be staying there long, she felt, no more than a year or two, and then she would take off for California and get herself a job in the wardrobe department at one of the Hollywood studios. Imagine that, she would tell the young Baumgartner: making dresses for one of those big costume dramas about the Napoleonic Wars or fitting Carole Lombard for the slinky, shimmering gown she would be wearing in the scene when she walks into the smoky New York nightclub with William Powell. Wouldn't that have been *just fabulous*? Yes, Baumgartner would say, *just fabulous*, but every time he was about to tell her that he wished she had gone ahead and done it, he realized that he never would have been born if she had, and so, rather than say anything more, he would just sit there and smile at her.

After his father's death, during that weird week back on Lyons Avenue when the two of them sat up late every night talking in the kitchen, Baumgartner urged his mother to sell the shop, sell the building, and get out of there. Put that money together with the life insurance money, and she would have enough to go anywhere she wanted. She was only forty-six, still young, still vibrant, and a hundred possible futures were still open to her. Newark was going down, he said, and it wouldn't be long before the city fell to pieces, and if she took the bull by the horns and acted now, she would be gone before the worst of it started to happen.

I'm not saying you're wrong, Sy, but where would I go? Naomi's still in school, and I have to think about her first, don't I?

You don't have to go far. Just cross the city line and move to Maplewood, or South Orange, or West Orange, or Montclair. All those towns have good schools, and poor Naomi would be a lot happier in one of those places than where she is now. There's no conflict. By leaving for yourself, you'll be leaving for her, too. And you'll finally be rid of this crummy apartment.

If I shut down the store, what happens to Bella? And Cookie Castellanos? And Mary Bolton, the Negro girl we hired in September? It's her first job, and she's doing so well, how can I just kick her out on the street?

Bella's already on Social Security, she'll have Medicare before you know it, since the bill is bound to pass sometime this year, and those grown-up nieces of hers, Dingbat and Doofus, can fill up the slack. As for Cookie and Mary, if someone wants to take over the store, put it in the contract that they have to be kept on the payroll. And if the person who buys the building wants to shut down the store, there's nothing you can do but give them large severance checks—no less than six months' pay—and wish them luck. They're both young, and they'll land on their feet before long.

You make it sound so simple.

That's because it is simple.

And what happens to me? What am I supposed to do out there in a big suburban house, waiting for Naomi to come home from school? Vacuum the rugs? Play solitaire? Take up booze and turn into a lush? I've always worked, Sy, I've been working since I was sixteen, seventeen years old, and running this store is my whole life. I know you don't think much of it, and I know that a part of your father always hated it, but even if Trocadero Fashions is a run-of-the-mill dress shop for unfashionable women, those women are real people, and they deserve to walk around feeling good about themselves. That's what I've been doing all these years, taking those run-of-the-mill dresses and redesigning them in the alterations so they'll hang right and be cut along the right lines so those women will look attractive in them, and if you feel attractive, you feel good about yourself, and to make those lumpy, middle-aged women feel good about themselves is a service, isn't it, what I would call a mitzvah, and so I feel proud of what I've done here, Sy, and don't feel I've wasted my talents on something that isn't worth the trouble, since every person is worth the trouble, no matter who that person is.

I know that, Ma. It's just that I think it's time to throw in the towel. The shop is one thing, but there's also the problem of Newark, and before you know it, all those women you've been helping are going to move away, and then what happens to you and the shop and Naomi and everything else you care about? Move, I'm begging you, sell out and move, and once you settle in somewhere, go back to work and keep on working for as long as you want. Remember your old dream about getting a job in a Hollywood studio? Well, those studios are dead now, aren't they, but if you want to design costumes, there's a lot going on in the New York theaters these days, not just Broadway but Off Broadway and Off Off Broadway and Off Off Off Broadway, and I'm sure you could hook up with someone in the city and start doing that, but if theater is too steep a hill to climb just now, think back to Madame Rosalie and remember that all her clients used to come from the suburban towns I've just mentioned along with about twenty-seven others and that there are a lot of people in those towns with money, and if you opened up your own shop in one of those places close to where they live, I'll bet you dollars to doughnuts they'll all come running, and before you know it you'll have more work than you can handle.

Baumgartner's mother started to laugh. For the first time since his father's funeral, laughter was pouring from her throat, and then she said: Remember the wedding gown I was commissioned to make a few years ago?

How could I forget it? I don't think I've ever laughed so hard in my life.

I'm sorry I did that to you, Sy, but there was no one else I could turn to. Cookie was too short, and the girl who came before Mary was too fat. There was a deadline, and I had to get the dress ready for the final fitting with the bride. How old were you then?

Fourteen.

Fourteen, and you were starting to shoot up, somewhere around five-five or five-six by then, which was the same height as the girl, who also happened to be thin, about the same size and shape you were at the time, minus the boobs, of course, and so I asked if you'd be willing to wear the dress while I made the adjustments I needed to make. At first you said no, but when I asked again, you said, All right, if it's really that important. And the nice thing about it is that you didn't get angry at me. You put on the dress, and two seconds later you collapsed in a fit of the giggles.

I was thinking about that funny movie we saw when I was eleven or twelve. *Some Like It Hot*, with Jack Lemmon and Tony Curtis prancing around in dresses and sexy Marilyn Monroe spilling out of a dress that made her look half-naked, and there I was in Susan Schwartzman's wedding dress, laughing my head off because I felt so embarrassed and confused, and just when we were about to finish, in walked you-know-who.

He must have heard you laughing, so he came downstairs to see what was going on.

And said: God damn it, Ruth, what the hell are you doing to the boy!

And you said, so help me: Don't worry, Dad, we're doing *Some Like It Hot* at school, and I'm rehearsing for tomorrow's audition. Which one do you think I should go for, Jack Lemmon or Tony Curtis?

And for the fifth or sixth time in all the years I'd known him, the old man burst out laughing.

And when he stopped, he looked at us and said: Well, nobody's perfect.

And then calmly walked back upstairs.

For the third or fourth time this afternoon, Baumgartner stops in mid-thought and looks up. A thick cloud has passed in front of the sun, temporarily darkening the sky, and with this sudden change in the atmosphere, Baumgartner looks around the yard to reconnect with his surroundings or to digest what he has been thinking about, he isn't quite sure which one, and realizes that the chair is uncomfortable, that his back hurts and that his legs are growing stiff, so he stands up and stretches out his arms for a few moments and shakes his legs one after the other and then bends down to touch his toes, which he hasn't been able to do for several years now, but even if the tips of his fingers can descend no farther than mid-shin, the effort itself is a welcome relief from the immobility of sitting stock-still in the uncomfortable chair, so he straightens up and bends down again, then does it again one last time. By now, the cloud has moved on and the sun is no longer blocked, but the light has changed somewhat, a subtle, barely noticeable change that has given the light a deeper, more sharply defined texture, and as Baumgartner walks around the yard looking for a better chair to sit in, assuming there is one, he realizes that the advancing afternoon has moved a bit more rapidly than he had thought, that the moment will soon be coming when the sun declines into an even more acute angle and the world it shines upon will be bathed in a spectral beauty of glowing, breathing things that will slowly dim and vanish into darkness when night falls. Meanwhile, Baumgartner is testing out another chair, which proves to be more uncomfortable than the first. He tests out another but rejects that one as well, and then he goes back to the first chair, which turns out to be less uncomfortable than he had thought, so he settles in again with another round of slow, methodical breathing and asks himself where his mind will be taking him next.

His thoughts jump to an image of Anna's face, Anna's face in tears as she walks into the living room of his mother's house to tell him that his mother has just died. After sitting by her hospice bed for twelve straight hours, Baumgartner had gone off to the sofa in the living room for a short nap, but Anna, who had napped earlier, stayed on in the bedroom, and she was the one who had watched his mother die. Pancreatic cancer. Six brutal months as her small body shrank to an appalling thinness, and now she was dead at sixty-two.

Until the cancer, she had made a new life for herself, selling the Lyons Avenue operation in 1966, eighteen months after his father's death and one year before his prophecy about Newark came true—in ways far more deadly and violent than he ever imagined it would. By then, his mother had settled into a little two-story house in Montclair with Naomi, the obstinate, floundering, often miserable Naomi who nevertheless began to settle down somewhat in her last two years of high school, and sometime around then, in 1969 he thinks it was, the opening of Madame Ruth's, which specialized in sumptuous wedding gowns for girls with wealthy parents but also made other sorts of clothes for both men and women, with the added bonus that Cookie and Mary came back to work for her and stayed on even after they found husbands and started having children, so Cookie and Mary were often in the house with them during the last weeks of his mother's life, as was Naomi, who was married by then and had a one-year-old girl. His mother died too young, well before she had a chance to become an old woman, but she lived long enough to have known Anna for years, to have loved Anna for years, and long enough to have known and loved her baby granddaughter, Barbara. In all that time, there were no men, not even a date with anyone as far as Baumgartner knew, let alone any thought of ever wanting to marry again. For several years in the 1970s, she seemed to have formed a close friendship with an older woman named Maggie Waldman, but the nature of that friendship was never clear to Baumgartner. For her sake, he hopes the two of them fell in love, but Maggie Waldman died three years before his mother did, and he will never know what happened or didn't happen between them.

His thoughts drift from the end of his mother's life to the beginning of her life and then push on back to the years and centuries before that, and suddenly he is remembering his trip to Ukraine two years ago and the day he spent in the town where her father was born. He had been invited to take part in some panel discussions at PEN International's annual congress, which was being held in Lviv that year, and not only did he want to participate in the panels and meet representatives of PEN chapters from around the world, he knew there would be enough time to take an afternoon off and travel two hours to the south and visit his grandfather's town. Some extraordinary things happened to him during that visit, things he has wanted to write about ever since he came home but has not gotten around to because he has been busy with his book, but now, with memories of his mother burning in his mind, he abruptly stands up from the chair, walks back into the house, and returns to the second-floor workroom he left an hour and a half ago. Pushing aside the drafts and corrections and notes related to *Mysteries of the Wheel*, he suspends work on his book and begins to write an account of his journey to Ivano-Frankivsk on September 21, 2017. He works for several hours and doesn't stop until his stomach calls him downstairs for dinner, then picks it up again the next day and works until dinnertime that evening as well. He seems to have finished, he thinks, but just to make sure, he goes back to it the next morning and spends three more hours eradicating typos and blunders, improving the rhythms of the prose, and putting the final touches on his short, confounding text.

THE WOLVES OF STANISLAV

Does an event have to be true in order to be accepted as true, or does belief in the truth of an event already make it true, even if the thing that supposedly happened did not happen? And what if, in spite of your efforts to find out whether the event took place or not, you arrive at an impasse of uncertainty and cannot be sure if the story someone told you on the terrace of a café in the western Ukrainian city of Ivano-Frankivsk was derived from a little known but verifiable historical event or was a legend or a boast or a groundless rumor passed on from a father to a son? Even more to the point: If the story turns out to be so astounding and so powerful that your jaw drops open and you feel that it has changed or enhanced or deepened your understanding of the world, does it matter if the story is true or not?

Circumstances led me to Ukraine in September 2017. My business was in Lviv, but I took advantage of an off-day to travel two hours to the south and spend the afternoon in Ivano-Frankivsk, where my maternal grandfather had been born sometime in the early 1880s. There was no reason to go there except curiosity, or else what I would call the lure of a counterfeit nostalgia, for the fact was that I had never known my grandfather and still know next to nothing about him. He died twenty-seven years before I was born, a shadow-man from the unwritten, unremembered past, and even as I traveled to the city he had left in the late nineteenth or early twentieth century, I understood that the place where he had spent his boyhood and adolescence was no longer the place where I would be spending the afternoon. Still, I wanted to go there, and as I look back and ponder the reasons why I wanted to go, perhaps it comes down to a single verifiable fact: The journey would be taking me through the bloodlands of Eastern Europe, the central horror-zone of twentieth-century slaughter, and if the shadow-man responsible for giving my mother her name had not left that part of the world when he did, I never would have been born.

What I already knew in advance of my arrival was that before it became Ivano-Frankivsk in 1962 (in honor of Ukrainian poet Ivan Franko), the four-hundred-year-old city had been known variously as Stanislawów, Stanislau, Stanislaviv, and Stanislav, depending on whether it had been under Polish, German, Ukrainian, or Soviet rule. A Polish city had become a Hapsburg city, a Hapsburg city had become an Austro-Hungarian city, an Austro-Hungarian city had become a Russian city in the first two years of World War I, then an Austro-Hungarian city, then a Ukrainian city for a short time after the war, then a Polish city, then a Soviet city (from September 1939 to July 1941), then a German-controlled city (until July 1944), then a Soviet city, and now, following the collapse of the Soviet Union in 1991, a Ukrainian city. At the time of my grandfather's birth, the population was 18,000, and in 1900 (the approximate year of his departure) there were 26,000 people living there, more than half of them Jews. By the time of my visit, the population had grown to 230,000, but back during the years of the Nazi occupation the number had been somewhere between eighty and ninety-five thousand, half Jewish, half non-Jewish, and what I had already known for several decades by then is that after the German invasion in the summer of 1941, ten thousand Jews had been rounded up and shot in the

Jewish cemetery that fall and by December the remaining Jews had been herded into a ghetto, from which ten thousand more Jews had been shipped off to the Belżec death camp in Poland, and then, one by one and five by five and twenty by twenty throughout 1942 and early 1943, the Germans had marched the surviving Jews of Stanislau into the woods surrounding the city and had shot them and shot them and shot them until there were no Jews left—tens of thousands of people murdered by a bullet to the back of the head and then buried in the common pits that had been dug by the murdered ones before they were killed.

A kind woman I had met in Lviv took charge of organizing the trip for me, and because she had been born and raised in Ivano-Frankivsk and still lived there, she knew where to go and what to see and even went to the trouble of enlisting someone to drive us there. A young lunatic with no fear of death, the driver barreled down the narrow two-lane highway as if he were auditioning for a stuntman's job in a racing-car movie, taking inordinate risks to pass every vehicle in front of us as he calmly and abruptly swerved into the other lane even as oncoming cars hurtled toward us from the opposite direction, and several times during the trip it occurred to me that this dull, overcast afternoon on the first day of autumn 2017 would be my last day on earth, and how ironic it was, I said to myself, and yet how terribly fitting, that I should have come all this way to visit the city my grandfather had left more than a hundred years ago only to die before I got there.

Fortunately, the traffic was sparse, a mix of fast-moving cars and slow-moving trucks and, at one point, a horse-drawn wagon loaded down with a massive pile of hay, moving at one-tenth the speed of the slowest-moving trucks. Stout, thick-legged women with babushkas on their heads trudged along the side of the road carrying plastic bags filled with groceries. Except for the plastic bags, they could have been figures from two hundred years ago, Eastern European peasant women trapped in a past so old and so durable that it had lived on into the twenty-first century. We passed through the outskirts of a dozen small towns as large, recently harvested fields stretched out on either side of us, but then, about two-thirds of the way there, the rural landscape dissolved into a no-man's-land of heavy industry, the most spectacular example being the gargantuan power plant that suddenly rose up before us on our left. If I have not scrambled what the kind woman told me in the car, that monolithic installation supplies Germany and other Western European countries with the bulk of their electricity. Such are the contradictory truths of that eight-hundred-mile-wide buffer state locked in the slaughter-lands between East and West, for even as Ukraine feeds one side with the electrical juice to light the lights and keep things running, on the other side it goes on spilling blood to defend its shrinking, embattled territory.

Ivano-Frankivsk turned out to be an attractive place, a city that bore no resemblance to the disintegrating urban ruin I had pictured in my mind. The clouds had dispersed just minutes before we got there, and with the sun shining and scores of people walking around in the streets and public squares, I was impressed by how clean and well-ordered it was, not some provincial backwater stuck in the past but a small contemporary city with bookstores, theaters, restaurants, and a pleasing blend of new and old architecture, the old having survived in the seventeenth- and eighteenth-century buildings constructed by the Polish founders and their Hapsburg conquerors. I would have been content to wander around for two or three hours and then head back, but the kind woman who had orchestrated the visit understood that my purpose in going there had been connected to my grandfather, and because my grandfather had been a Jew, she thought it might be helpful for me to talk with the one rabbi left in town, the spiritual leader of Ivano-Frankivsk's last remaining synagogue—which proved to be a solid, handsomely designed building from the first years of the twentieth century that had somehow managed to come through the Second World War with only minor damage, all of which had long since been repaired. I'm not sure what I thought, but I had no objection to talking to the rabbi, since he was probably the only person still aboveground anywhere in the world who might—just might—have been able to tell me something about my family, that nameless horde of invisible ancestors who had scattered and died and subsequently vanished from the realm of the knowable, for it was all but certain that their birth records had been destroyed by a bomb or a fire or the signature of some overzealous bureaucrat at some point in the past hundred years. Talking to the rabbi would be a useless errand, I realized, a by-product of the counterfeit nostalgia that had brought me to the city in the first place, but there I was, there for that day and that day only, with no thought of ever coming back, and what harm would it do to ask some questions and see if any of them could be answered?

There were no answers. The bearded, Orthodox rabbi welcomed us into his office, but beyond telling me what I had already known—that Auster was a name common among the Jews of Stanislav and nowhere else—and then digressing briefly into a story from the war about a woman named Auster who had eluded capture by the Germans by hiding in a hole for three years and then emerging from the hole insane, a mad person for the rest of her life—he had no information to give me. A hectic, jittery man who chain-smoked ultra-thin cigarettes throughout the conversation, stubbing them out after just a few puffs and then pulling fresh ones from a plastic bag on his desk, he was neither friendly nor unfriendly, simply distracted, a man with other things on his mind and, as far as I could tell, too busy with his own concerns to show much interest in his American visitor or the woman who had arranged the meeting. By most accounts, there are no more than two or three hundred Jews living in Ivano-Frankivsk today. It is unclear how many of them practice their religion or attend services at the synagogue, but from what I had witnessed an hour before I met the rabbi, it would seem that no more than a small fraction of that diminished number take part. By pure chance, my visit happened to fall on Rosh Hashanah, one of the most sacred days on the liturgical calendar, and only fifteen people had been present in the sanctuary to listen to the sounding of the shofar that welcomes in the new year, thirteen men and two women. Unlike their counterparts in Western Europe and America on such occasions, the men had not been wearing dark suits and ties but nylon windbreakers, and their heads had been covered by red and yellow baseball caps.

We went back outside and wandered around for an hour, an hour and a half, perhaps longer. The kind woman had arranged for me to talk with another person at four o'clock, a poet from Ivano-Frankivsk who had apparently spent years delving into the city's history, but for now there was time to explore some of the places we had missed earlier, and so we pushed on with our rambles until we had covered a large part of the city. The sun was blazing by then, and in that beautiful September light we drifted onto a large, open square and found ourselves standing in front of the Church of the Holy Resurrection, an eighteenth-century baroque cathedral that is considered to be the most beautiful Hapsburg structure from the years when Ivano-Frankivsk had been known as Stanislau. As was the case with other beautiful churches and cathedrals I had visited in Western European towns and cities, I assumed it would be mostly empty when we walked in, with no one about except for some random tourists and their cameras. I was wrong. This was not Western Europe, after all, it was the far western edge of what had once been the Soviet Union, a city located in the province of Galicia at the far eastern edge of the former Austro-Hungarian Empire, and the church, which was not Roman Catholic or Russian Orthodox but Greek Catholic, was crammed with people, none of them tourists or scholars of baroque architecture but local citizens who had come to pray or to think or to commune with themselves or the Almighty in that vast stone space with September light pouring through the stained-glass windows. There must have been about two hundred of them in all, and what struck me most about that large, silent crowd was how many young people were in it, a good half of the total number, men and women in their early twenties sitting in pews with their heads bowed or on their knees with their hands clasped and their heads turned upward and their eyes fixed on the light pouring through the stained-glass windows. An ordinary weekday afternoon, with nothing to distinguish it from any other day except that the weather had become exceptionally fine, and on that radiant afternoon the Church of the Holy Resurrection was full of young people who were neither at work nor sitting around in outdoor cafés but kneeling on the stone floor with their hands clasped and their heads turned upward in postures of prayer. The chain-smoking rabbi, the red and yellow baseball caps, and now this.

And after this, which had come after that, it made perfect sense to me that the poet should have turned out to be a Buddhist. And no, he was not some New Age convert who had read a couple of books about Zen but a longtime practitioner who had just returned from a four-month stay at a monastery in Nepal, a serious man. And also a poet, and also a student of the city in which my grandfather had been born. He was a large, hulking fellow with meaty hands and an affable manner, a clear-eyed, thoughtful person dressed in European clothes who mentioned his commitment to Buddhism only in passing, which I took to be an encouraging sign, and therefore I trusted him and felt I could depend on him to tell me the truth. The meeting took place just two years ago, but the odd thing about our encounter is that even after such a short time and even though I have thought about it almost every day since, I am unable to remember a single thing he told me about the city before he mentioned the wolves. Once he began to tell that story, everything else was erased.

We were sitting on the terrace of a café looking out at the largest square in the city, the central hub of Stanislau-Stanislav-Ivano-Frankivsk, a broad space awash in sunlight with no cars and a great many people walking from here to there in all directions, not one of them making a sound as I remember it, nothing but a mass of silent bodies passing in front of me as I listened to the poet tell the story. We had already established the fact that I was familiar with what had happened to the Jewish half of the population between 1941 and 1943, but when the Soviet army rolled in to capture the city in July 1944, he said, just six weeks after the Allied invasion of Normandy, not only had the Germans already cleared out but the other half of the population was gone as well. They had all run off in one direction or another, east or west, north or south, which meant that the Soviets had conquered an empty city, a domain of nothingness. The human population had dispersed to the four winds, and instead of people the city was now inhabited by wolves, hundreds of wolves, hundreds upon hundreds of wolves.

Horrible, I thought, so horrible that it contained the horror of the most horrible dream, and suddenly, as if rising up from a dream of my own, the poem by Georg Trakl came rushing back to me—"Eastern Front," which I had first read fifty years earlier, had read again and again until I knew it by heart and then had retranslated for myself, the World War I poem from 1914 written about

Gródek, a Galician city not far from Stanislau that ends
with the stanza:

> A thorn-studded wilderness girds the city.
> From bloody stairs the moon
> Chases terrified women.
> Wild wolves have stormed through the gates.

How did he know this? I asked.

His father, he said, his father had told him about it
many times, and then he went on to explain that his father
had been a young man in 1944, barely into his twenties,
and after the Soviets took control of Stanislau, henceforth
to be known as Stanislav, he had been conscripted into
an army unit assigned to the task of exterminating the
wolves. The job took several weeks, he said, or perhaps it
was several months, I can't remember, and once Stanislav
was fit for human habitation again, the Soviets repopu-
lated the city with military personnel and their families.

I looked out at the square in front of me and tried to
imagine it in the summer of 1944, all the people walking around on their errands from here to there suddenly
gone, expunged from the scene, and then I began to see
the wolves, dozens of wolves loping through the square,
moving along in small packs as they searched for food in
the abandoned city. The wolves are the endpoint of the
nightmare, I said to myself, the farthest outcome of the
stupidity that leads to the devastations of war, in this case

the three million Jews murdered in those eastern blood-lands along with countless other civilians and soldiers from other religions or no religion, and once the slaughter has ended, wild wolves come crashing through the gates of the city. The wolves are not just symbols of war. They are the spawn of war and what war brings to the earth.

I have no doubt that the poet believed he was telling me the truth. The wolves were real to him, and because of the calm conviction in his voice as he told the story, I accepted them as real myself. Admittedly, he had not seen the wolves with his own eyes, but his father had, and why would a father tell his son such a story if it hadn't been true? He wouldn't, I told myself, and when I left Ivano-Frankivsk later that afternoon, I was convinced that for a short time after the Russians had taken control of Stanislav from the Germans, wolves had ruled the city.

In the weeks and months that followed, I did what I could to investigate the matter more thoroughly. I talked to a friend who had contacts with historians at the university in Lviv (formerly known as Lvov, Lwów, and Lemberg), in particular one woman who specialized in the history of the region, but in none of her past research had she ever stumbled across anything about the wolves of Stanislav, she said, and when she looked into the matter more thoroughly herself, she failed to turn up a single reference to the story the poet had told. What she did turn up, however, was a short film that documents the capture of the city by Soviet troops on July 27, 1944, and when a video of that film was sent to me, I was able to watch it for myself as I sat in the same chair I am sitting in now.

Fifty or a hundred soldiers in neatly ordered ranks march into Stanislav as a small crowd of well-dressed, well-fed citizens cheers their arrival. The scene then plays out again from a slightly different angle, showing the same fifty or a hundred soldiers and the same well-dressed, well-fed crowd. The film then cuts away to an image of a collapsed bridge, and then, before it dribbles to its conclusion, cuts back to the original shot of the soldiers and the cheering crowd. The soldiers might have been genuine soldiers, but in this instance they had been asked to play the role of soldiers, just as the actors who had been directed to play the cheering crowd were performing their roles in a crudely edited, unfinished propaganda film intended to glorify the goodness and valor of the Soviet Union.

Needless to say, not one wolf appears anywhere in the film.

Which brings me back to the place where I began and the question that has no answer: What to believe when you can't be sure whether a supposed fact is true or not true?

In the absence of any information that could confirm or deny the story he told me, I choose to believe the poet. And whether they were there or not, I choose to believe in the wolves.

5

For the time being, everything has stopped. Baumgartner has written the last sentence of the last paragraph of the last chapter of *Mysteries of the Wheel*, and now, for the next month or so, he must forget that the book is done or that he ever took it upon himself to write such a book in the first place. Baumgartner refers to this post-composition period as the *collapse*, or *Mrs. Dolittle in her cups*, or, echoing the tagline of the old Coca-Cola ad from his childhood, *the pause that refreshes*. It is the fundamental next step toward the completion of a book, for after living with the book-in-progress every day and every night for what can amount to several years or even many years, you are so close to it by the time you finish that you can no longer judge what you have done. More than that, the words you have written are so familiar to you by then that they have gone dead on the page, and to look at them now would engulf you in such spasms of disgust that you might feel tempted to destroy the manuscript in a fit of rage or despair. For your own sanity, and for the sake of whatever might be salvageable from the disaster you have wrought, you must force yourself to step back and leave the damned thing alone until it has become so thoroughly detached from you that once you dare to pick it up again, you will feel that you are encountering it for the first time.

One of the many lessons learned over the years by the old lifer still serving out his sentence in the last occupied cell on the third floor of Correctional Facility No. 7.

For the time being, therefore, everything has stopped, and Baumgartner has come to another one of his periodic interludes of enforced idleness. More often than not, he has tended to use those blanks to take care of mundane, practical tasks, all the dreary obligations of day-to-day life that he willfully ignores and leaves undone whenever he is hard at work on a project. Going to the dentist, for example, or buying some new clothes for himself, or, after putting it off for a year and a half, calling the doctor's office to schedule his long-deferred annual checkup, or attending to various eyesores in the house, such as the post-Kierkegaardian purge that finally eradicated the mess on the back porch when he hired a local guy known as The Man with a Van to cart his unwanted books to the public library—the contents of four hundred and twelve cardboard packages handed to him by the valiant Molly, the luminous being from UPS who has outlasted all the other women who have walked in and out of his life over the past ten years.

This time is different from all those other times, however, and Baumgartner is ablaze with plans, bold plans that go far beyond the customary business of having his teeth cleaned or buying a new pair of shoes. It has been four days since he wrote the last sentence of his book. Immediately after that, he printed out a copy of the two-hundred-and-sixty-one-page manuscript and put it in a drawer of his desk, telling himself not to look at it again for another month or six weeks, that is, not until the middle or the end of November. Then, two days after that (October 17, 2019), which was just two days ago, something unexpected happened, and on the strength of that something, a buoyant, newly inspired Baumgartner has rolled up his sleeves and plunged into the work of meeting the challenge it presents.

The surprise came in the form of a letter sent from Ann Arbor, Michigan. A proper letter of two single-spaced typed pages mailed directly to Baumgartner's Poe Road address in a standard business-size envelope from a person named Beatrix Coen. *Dear Professor Baumgartner*, it began, followed by an opening paragraph that explained how Ms. Coen happened to have Baumgartner's private address, which had been passed on to her by their mutual friend, Tom Nozwitszki, her faculty adviser in the graduate program of English and Comparative Literature at the University of Michigan. Dear old Tom of the frizzy hair and protruding gut, Baumgartner said to himself, their chatterboxing pal from the New School days in the late seventies and early eighties, a bit younger than they were and half in love with Anna, a relentless, harmless flirt but always sharp, invigorating to talk to, American poetry man, contemporary stuff, the renegades and outliers from the Black Mountain crowd, the New York School, and all the rest, off to Ann Arbor around the same time Baumgartner and Anna moved to Princeton and author of the longest, most probing, and enthusiastic review of Anna's book. Tom Nozwitszki, who is still in touch from time to time and never fails to call Baumgartner when he comes to New York and, as it happens, sent Baumgartner an email last week to vouch for Ms. Coen and to give STB a heads-up that her letter would be arriving soon, but Baumgartner had missed the email in the swarm of messages cluttering his inbox, scores of unread and neglected communications shunted to the dark edge of consciousness as he was pushing on through the last chapter of his book. So he read Ms. Coen's letter before he read what Tom had to say about her (a brilliant young woman . . . my best student in years . . . a beautiful thinker and writer who loves Anna's poems and—how strange is this?—sometimes makes me think of Anna herself . . .), but the truth was that Ms. Coen's letter was strong enough to stand as its own endorsement, and by the time Baumgartner read the last sentence, he knew that he had to answer her at once.

She was hoping to do her dissertation on Anna's work, but since that work came down to just one book of a hundred and twelve pages, she doubted the committee would accept her proposal. Which explained why she was writing to Baumgartner now: to find out whether there was more work beyond the eighty-eight poems published in *Lexicon*. More poems to begin with, but also any prose writings that might be on hand, or letters, or a journal of some kind, or notebooks, or working drafts and revisions, or any other unpublished material that would help her come to a fuller understanding of *Anna Blume's disconcerting genius*. Baumgartner grinned when he read those words. Then he thwacked his hand on the kitchen table and put down the letter for a moment to exult. This girl was serious, he said to himself, and she was asking all the right questions. If there were indeed any unpublished manuscripts, she continued, she wanted to know if he had turned them over to an archive somewhere or if (as Tom Nozwitszki suspected) the papers were still in his house on Poe Road, and if they were there, she wondered if he would allow her to come for a visit and to hang around long enough to go through all the material he had—assuming that could be accomplished in a single visit. She would find her own lodgings, of course, and she would follow whatever rules he imposed on her: so many hours a day, for example, and specifically designated times for asking questions, so she wouldn't interfere with his work or make a nuisance of herself.

There had been many letters in the years since Anna's book was published, but nothing quite like this one, which was not an anthology request or a translation inquiry or an emotionally charged fan letter from a lonely high school girl in Massachusetts or Nebraska but the promise of a yearslong commitment from a talented young scholar to write the first full-length study of the Blumian mind in all its manifold incarnations. Baumgartner was unaccountably moved by this. It was more than happiness, he realized, more than just a cause for celebration, but a feeling of destiny fulfilled, somehow, as if, without ever consciously knowing it, Baumgartner had been waiting for such a letter ever since Redwing Press published Anna's book nine years ago, not actively expecting it, perhaps, but hoping there was someone out there in the vast mysterium of human others who would care enough about what Anna had given the world to sit down and write that letter to him. Now the letter had arrived, and not only did Baumgartner understand that his empty, no-Judith existence of the past year would soon be coming to an end but that nearly everything else about his life was about to change as well.

Needless to say, there were voluminous quantities of unpublished material for Beatrix Coen to study, and needless to say, Baumgartner had every intention of inviting her to the house and allowing her to *hang around* in his presence for as long as she wanted or needed to be there. At the same time, he began to worry that a twenty-seven-year-old graduate student would not be able to afford the snob prices of the inns, hotels, and bed-and-breakfasts in and around Princeton, and when he considered the bleak Motel 6 alternatives on the noisy, cluttered highways elsewhere in the general area, he concluded that it would be better for her pocketbook and his peace of mind if she camped out with him. Not in the house, however, since there are only three bedrooms on the second floor, one of which he sleeps in himself, one of which has been turned into his study, and the last of which is the little guest room right next door to his room, a proximity that would cause no end of awkwardness and embarrassment for Baumgartner's visitor, not to speak of Baumgartner himself: two strangers sharing a single bathroom and forced to bunk down each night within six feet of each other on either side of the thin wall between them. If Baumgartner rolls onto his back at any point during the night, he will inevitably snore, and who knows if the young Ms. Coen doesn't snore as well? On the other hand, there is the apartment under the eaves of the two-car garage, a pleasant little space large enough to house two people, with a bed, a chest of drawers, an armoire, a kitchenette, a bathroom with a stall shower, and a freestanding, jumbo-sized electric heater. He and Anna used to rent it out to graduate students for the first five or six years they lived there, and when they no longer needed the extra money, they kept it available for long-term and weekend visits from their New York friends. Since Anna's death, Baumgartner has more or less forgotten about the apartment, and if not for the conscientious Mrs. Flores, who insists on putting the place through rigorous spring and fall cleanings every year, the once attractive loft would have turned into an empire of bats and spiders and dust. As it is, a few weeks of touch-ups and repair work should be enough to get it back into shape, and on October seventeenth, roughly six hours after he finished reading Beatrix Coen's letter, Baumgartner hired Mr. Flores and his crew to do the job. To be followed by a second job inside the house after the first job was done: to dismantle the old staircase leading down to the basement and build a new one from scratch. At last.

That same day, he called Tom Nozwitszki in Ann Arbor. After running through the obligatory hellos and how-are-yous and what-have-you-been-up-to-lateleys, Baumgartner said: Tell me something more about your Beatrix Coen. I understand from your note that she's uncommonly gifted and promising, but I'm about to invite her to come here for what could turn out to be an extended visit, and I need to know if she's a stable, reasonably grounded person who won't bring disaster and misery into my house. There's a ton of material I'm willing to share with her, but if she turns out to be cracked, or inordinately difficult, or too shy or too talkative or too demanding or too something else, I'll change my plans and figure out another way to deal with her. Assuming I want to deal with her at all.

Tom laughed. Don't worry, Sy. She's a solid girl. Highly intelligent, pleasant to be with, poised. *One of us*, as Conrad used to say. I've known her for three years, and I've always found her to be steady, serious, and hardworking, but also funny when she's in the right mood, zany-funny, the way Anna could be when she went off on one of her jags, which is why I sometimes think of Anna when Bebe's around.

Bebe?

That's what everyone calls her. And believe me, she's not your standard American issue. One-half Jewish, one-quarter WASP, and one-quarter black. Her maternal grandmother—who happened to be one of the first black women doctors in Philadelphia. On the other side, her paternal grandmother was the first Jewish woman to work in the physics department at Columbia. It's quite a pedigree, no? Big brains everywhere, but Bebe likes to refer to herself as a mongrel, or, as she once put it to me, *an anyone masquerading as everyone*. What else? An art historian mother and a biochemist father who both teach at the University of Chicago, and a couple of siblings wandering around somewhere in America or Europe or both. Also, just to reassure you, she's read most of your books or maybe all of your books and thinks you're the best thing going since Wheaties.

Breakfast of champions.

That was the implication, although she didn't come out and say it in so many words.

After the conversation with Tom, Baumgartner sent off his response to Ann Arbor, and with that letter he and Beatrix Coen started making plans for her visit and the many days or weeks or even months it will take for her to plow through the twelve hundred pages of Anna's unpublished manuscripts and letters. The old man is immensely grateful to the young woman for her passionate interest in Anna's work, and the young woman is immensely grateful to the old man for his generosity in supporting her efforts and for going to the outlandish trouble and ridiculous expense of revamping the guest apartment over the garage for her sake, and so deep is the gratitude of each toward the other that in the early flow of emails and letters and postcards that sailed back and forth between them, one might have been fooled into thinking they were members of Louis's court at Versailles in the eighteenth century rather than a pair of twenty-first-century commoners from the ragged, disintegrating hinterlands of the New World, for *politesse* at the level they practiced it in their written exchanges was unheard of in the place and time they inhabited. Little by little, however, the high-flown talk has modulated into earthier, more direct forms of discourse, and the two of them have settled into what seems to be developing into a grand friendship. Baumgartner is thrilled.

She has academic obligations until the end of the semester and is planning to visit her parents over Christmas break, so they arrange for her to come to New Jersey in the first days of the new year, a two-and-a-half-month gap that will give Baumgartner time to finish the repair work on the house, begin reacquainting himself with Anna's manuscripts, and then, in a month or so, to read through the manuscript of *Mysteries of the Wheel*, after which he will make any and all necessary revisions and give the book to his agent, Maddy Lifton, who in turn will email it over to his American publisher, Heller Books, the company that Anna helped found in 1972 and which has been publishing Baumgartner's work for close to forty years.

Now that the visit is on, and now that Mr. Flores and his men have begun their work in the garage apartment, Baumgartner decides that something must be done about the backyard as well, where the denuded flower beds have turned into dismal outposts of weeds and decaying underbrush after eleven years of neglect, during which he has done nothing more than hire a succession of high school boys to mow the lawn during the spring and summer with the ancient, progressively rusting manual machine that he and Anna inherited from the previous owners of the house. With Bebe Coen on the verge of becoming a temporary resident of Poe Road, however, her future host has fallen under a spell of intense horticultural longing. Once upon a time, when Anna was in charge of running the house, the yard had flowers and shrubs in it, nothing too elaborate or burdensome to take care of but a nice little patch of ground for all that, a motley array of bright colors and contrasting shapes and various registers of green, and now that it is mid-October, the best time of the year for planting shrubs and bulbs, Baumgartner aims to go on the attack and root out every withered stalk and dead bush and replant the whole damned garden before the ground freezes over and winter is upon them.

Which brings Ed Papadopoulos back into the story after an absence of several chapters, the meter-reading ex-ballplayer who showed such kindness to Baumgartner on the day he fell down the stairs, the compassionate, good-hearted tower of brawn who returned to the house after work as he promised he would, armed with a large bag of ice for Baumgartner's knee and a fresh supply of lightbulbs for the basement, and wound up staying around to whip up a dinner for Baumgartner and then cleaned the kitchen afterward. The two of them have become friends in the year and a half since then, and in that time Baumgartner has attended the young man's wedding (to a vivacious blonde travel agent named Mitzi last spring), has treated the newlyweds to elaborate dinners at the area's best Chinese, Mexican, and Italian restaurants, and has supported Ed's decision to quit PSE&G and go to work for his father's landscaping business, even though Ed and his father have a somewhat troubled relationship, but it was clear to Baumgartner by then that the gentle, highly sensitive Ed was endowed with an instinctive feel for all living things and that spending his days digging around in gardens and nurturing plants and flowers and trees would be a rewarding way to earn his living and that the satisfaction it brought would more than compensate for the occasional run-in with his cranky, bullying father. Ed has been at it for almost a year now, and with Baumgartner suddenly in need of his professional help, Ed and two young apprentices have begun showing up every morning to over-haul the backyard and restore the garden to its bygone luster. Such is the routine now: Mr. Flores and his men shuttling in and out of the garage throughout the day as Ed and his men toil in the yard, and because the two worksites are within close range of each other, the two gangs often intersect as they move around on their overlapping turfs, one consisting of three men who speak Spanish among themselves and the other of three men who converse in English. Neither set of helpers is capable of talking to the other, but then there is Ed Papadopoulos, the ex-A-ball pitcher who made it his business to learn Spanish in order to communicate with his Latin American teammates, all those bewildered kids from the D.R. and Mexico and Panama and Venezuela trans-ported to Gringoland without knowing a word of English, and just like that Ed is talking to Angel Flores and his two subordinates in their native language, and for the first time in all the years he has known him, Baumgartner has seen the withheld, often grim-faced Mr. Flores smile and even burst out laughing. STB knows enough Spanish to under-stand that the yardman and the carpenter, who was born and raised in the Dominican Republic, are mostly talking baseball, and how remarkable it is, Baumgartner thinks, that big, galumphing Ed, one of the least remarkable men on earth, has a gift for spreading life wherever he happens to go.

Meanwhile, Baumgartner has gathered together all of Anna's papers and is digging through them again for the first time in years. After he made his choices about which poems should be included in *Lexicon*, he had stopped thinking about the rejected ones, convinced that they didn't measure up to the others and probably shouldn't be published. But what if he had been wrong, and what if the standards he had imposed on himself had been too harsh and narrowly conceived? He had wanted Anna's book to make a splash, and therefore he had confined himself to the poems of hers he considered to be masterpieces, the best eighty-eight out of the two hundred and sixteen he had found, and the book had indeed made a splash and has continued to make a splash among an ever-growing number of new readers, but not even the greatest poets have it in them to write only masterpieces, and perhaps he has done Anna a disservice by taking such a stringent approach. Now, as he pores over the one hundred and twenty-eight discarded poems, which amount to nearly two hundred and fifty pages of unknown, invisible work, he finds himself reading them through Beatrix Coen's eyes, imagining how she will react to these less than perfect but often magnificent things as he goes through the vicarious experience of living in her skin and feeling her excitement at the discovery of what will surely come across to her as a massive trove of sizzling, tumultuous splendor. He is a true and proper idiot, Baumgartner says to himself, and what on earth had he been thinking by not putting together a second collection as a follow-up to *Lexicon*? A good seventy or eighty of these poems should be sent out into the world at once, if not all one hundred and twenty-eight of them for that matter, and at some point, who knows when, but at some point in the coming years, the two books should be combined and reconfigured into a large, one-volume collected poems—a monument of singing pages that will overwhelm the silence of Anna's grave.

There is more, however, much more. Not just Anna's autobiographical writings but translations of eighty-seven French, Spanish, and Portuguese poems that never found their way into print as well as three mountains of pen, pencil, and typewritten manuscripts of nearly all of Anna's poems, manuscripts of alternate drafts, most of them on sheets of eight-and-a-half-by-eleven paper but also on loose sheets torn from sketch pads, blank books, and lined notebooks of various dimensions, whether horizontally ruled American and British notebooks or quadralinear *cahiers* and *cuadernos* from France and Spain, along with poems or parts of poems scribbled on the backs of envelopes, electric bills, shopping lists, a roofer's invoice, and an eloquent, deeply felt note of thanks from the editor who published her translation of Lorca's *Poet in New York*. Also: manuscripts of a dozen book reviews and copies of the weekly and monthly magazines they

appeared in, five unpublished short stories, and the two hundred and thirty-six pages of Anna's two abandoned novels—
all of them crucial resources for Beatrix Coen's dissertation
(if she is allowed to write it) but not likely to be worth
publishing, given that both novels were left unfinished and
the five stories add up to just thirty pages. The translations
could be turned into a book, he feels, as could the fourteen
autobiographical texts (171 pages), but Baumgartner decides
not to decide just yet, and later on, when he thinks about
the matter again, he will act or not act only after consulting
with others, since he fears he could be getting carried away
with himself and doesn't want to blunder into a decision that
will do Anna and her work more harm than good.

Beyond moving forward with the poems, the only thing
he feels comfortable about trying to publish is his correspondence with Anna from mid-1969 to mid-1971, the two
hopelessly long years when they were stranded on opposite
sides of the Atlantic and had to stay in touch by letter or else
lose track of each other for good. They were still just babies
at the time—nineteen and twenty-one—and nothing solid
had been established between them, except perhaps the hope
that the small thing they had started together would eventually grow into a large thing and perhaps even a monumental
thing, although neither one of them dared to express that
hope when their separation began. Before that, there had
been the flubbed first sighting at the Goodwill Mission shop
in September, which could have been the end of the story

and most likely should have been, but eight months later they were given another chance, for contrary to what eminent rationalists have been telling us for years, the gods are happiest and most fully themselves when playing dice with the universe, and one afternoon at the end of May, Baumgartner happened to sit down at a table next to the one occupied by Anna at the Hungarian Pastry Shop on Amsterdam Avenue, not because he recognized her (her face was obscured by the book she was reading) but because it was the only free spot available to him. Anna described that second encounter in another one of her autobiographical pieces, *Early Days*:

Once he settled into his chair, the young man looked over at me and said: "I know you from somewhere, don't I?"

"*Know* might be an exaggeration," I replied, "but we did see each other once. Months and months ago at a secondhand store about ten blocks south of here. As I remember it, you were knee-deep in a barrel of pots."

"That's it!" he said. "The old rag-and-bone joint on Amsterdam and Ninety-eighth! We smiled at each other, didn't we?"

Immediately after he said the word *smile*, his face broke into another, much bigger smile than the one he had given me in the fall, and when I answered him with a much bigger smile of my own, I felt that something strange had just happened. Not the smiles, at least not in themselves, but the strange fact that we both should have remembered that small, fleeting moment from all those months ago, and the doubly strange fact that as a consequence of our shared memory of that moment we both should have been acting as if it had created a connection between us, when the truth was that we still knew nothing about each other. A little smile in the fall, a second chance encounter in the spring, and now a big smile—that was the extent of what had happened to us so far, and yet it was as if we had already known each other for some time by then, and perhaps we had, for it was obvious that we had each gone on thinking about the other from time to time over the many months between then and now, and now that fate had thrown us together for a second time, I sensed that we were equally determined not to screw up again by letting the moment pass.

Time was short, but from June to the middle of August they crammed in enough dates, dinners, long walks, movies, concerts, museums, and bone-shaking nights in bed for Baumgartner to conclude that Anna was a girl who stood apart from all the other girls he had ever known and to regret that he was about to take off for a year of philosophy courses at the Collège de France in Paris, no matter how much he had once been looking forward to it. Anna shared none of his certainties, however, and was even apprehensive about the strength of her attraction to him, for Baumgartner was on the verge of leaving New York from the minute they started talking to each other in the pastry shop that first afternoon and would no doubt forget all about her the moment he set foot on the plane. She was half in love with him in spite of that, but the other half of her knew she wasn't ready for an all-out, cataclysmic love, and even less ready because she was still suffering from the aftershocks of Frankie Boyle's eternally exploding body and the near-empty coffin that held his remains. Baumgartner adored her too much to press her into making declarations she wasn't prepared to make, and when he said good-bye to her on the last day, he held back from making any grand declarations of his own. He was no more ready at that point than Anna was for the Big Step, but secretly he was more confident than she was about the long term, since he already knew that his future life would be no life unless he could share it with her. Anna, however, had no such faith, and in their last hour together she even went so far as to insult him. You're a nasty little stinker, Sy, she said. You go on the offensive with one foot already out the door, and now that you've had your fun, it's bye-bye sweetheart, I'll be seeing you in my dreams.

More than that, Baumgartner said, I'll also be writing to you every day. And you'd better write back to me—or else.

Or else what?

I'll kick you out of my dreams.

You write, and I'll answer. But you're never going to write, so I won't have to worry about it, will I?

Don't be so sure, Miss Smarty Pants. If I were you, I'd start worrying now.

He didn't write every day, but by the time Anna came to Paris for a short visit in June 1970, the two of them had exchanged more than a hundred letters apiece, not one of them a love letter in the classic sense of the term, although from time to time they each referred to the hours they had spent in bed together the previous summer and how much they were looking forward to burning up the sheets again, which indeed happened during their electric, two-week reunion in Paris, after which Anna headed for a summer program in Madrid, and by the time she returned to Paris in August for a year at the Sorbonne, Baumgartner was packing his bags and preparing to return to New York. Bad luck, bad timing, bad whatever, but in any case a bizarre run of missed opportunities, and with Anna returning to Madrid for a second summer in 1971, another full year went by with an ocean standing between them. There was nothing for it but to go on writing letters to each other, somewhere between a hundred and twenty and a hundred and forty apiece over that last twelve-month stretch. Some of the letters are amusing (accounts of weird events from their daily lives), others are caustic, even bitter (political harangues against Nixon, Kissinger, and the ongoing war), but most of all the letters are an elaborate record of two young minds in transition, Anna's meticulous, outspoken, and often startling commentaries on the dead and living poets she was reading as she began to find a way toward the demotic, stripped-down language of her early style, Baumgartner grappling with and at last coming to the first clear articulations of his ideas about embodied consciousness and the doubleness of being that would go on haunting him for the next half century, and as their intimacy increased and their trust in each other grew, whole letters were given over to their doubts and innermost fears about themselves, which neither of them had ever shared with anyone else in the past. Still, much as they had come to depend on each other, no doubt love each other, these were not love letters but a correspondence between intellectual and spiritual comrades, soul mates who wisely made a pact at the beginning of their separation to ignore the absurd demands a vow of celibacy would have imposed on them, so a guiltless Baumgartner meandered through a number of casual flings in Paris and New York while Anna was in New York and Paris and hoped she had been doing the same in the cities where he hadn't been during their time apart. Curiously, he never got around to asking her whether she had or not, since Baumgartner strongly believed that what she did with her body was her own business and consequently none of his, and Anna, who also knew that his business was none of her business, never bothered to ask him.

It is November twenty-second now, the forty-seventh anniversary of Anna's run-in with death on Claremont Avenue. The two teams of workers have finished their jobs and are gone, Flores and Papadopoulos have been paid in full, and as Baumgartner muses about the long autobiographical essay he is planning to write about Anna as an introduction to their book of letters, he understands that he is thinking about his next project as a way to avoid dragging himself back into *Mysteries of the Wheel*, which he must start reading now in order to decide if it still needs more work, for if it does, he will have to get cracking and polish off the revisions before Beatrix Coen turns up on January fifth. Not because there is any deadline or because he couldn't go on tinkering with the manuscript for another year if he wanted to but because he is determined to *clear the decks* before she lands in Princeton and to put himself entirely at her disposal throughout the length of her visit, which will be all about Anna and her work and nothing but Anna and her work, and to savor the experience as fully as he wants to, Baumgartner must not be bogged down by his own work at the same time.

Fortunately, the book is not the out-and-out botch he feared it was. In fact, it isn't half bad and might even be considered good by some generous souls, but if you set out to make a work that borders on the ridiculous, and every sentence in that work oozes with self-mocking, double-edged ironies, you damned well better not slip up and lose your tone at any point in the text, for one false move will sabotage the deadly serious intentions hidden within the jokes and send the whole thing tumbling into a ravine of gibberish. As far as Baumgartner can tell, he hasn't slipped up in more than three or four places, each one fixable simply by crossing out the passage and removing it from the book, and therefore Baumgartner is more or less relieved, more or less not too disgusted with himself, even though the book is so fucking crazy that he can no longer understand how he managed to write it.

He can dimly recall Introduction to Philosophy, a course he took as a first-term student at Oberlin in which he read something by or about Aristotle that compared the body to a ship and the soul to the captain of that ship, which greatly amused Baumgartner at the time, since he found it impossible not to see the disembodied captain-soul as a flesh-and-blood captain standing behind the wheel of his human vessel and guiding it through treacherous waters in the China Seas, which made no sense, of course, given that a thing without substance (a soul) cannot be endowed with substance (a body) and still be called a soul. Nevertheless, if the Aristotelian self was a combination of matter and non-matter, that is, a visible body animated by an invisible soul, how interesting it would be to extend the metaphor and put the combined captain-soul and ship-body of an actual human being behind the wheel of a modern, motorized form of transportation, a twentieth-century car, for example, in which case the captain-soul at the helm of the ship-body would still be operating as a pure, insubstantial soul guiding a pure, physical car on its journey through space, but in that human beings are not pure souls or pure bodies but a combi-nation of the two, the driver of the car would necessarily be

a soul endowed with a body, or an embodied soul, a fact that
no card-carrying dualist would countenance, even if that fact
was repeated millions of times a day on millions of roads in all
parts of the world. Baumgartner had just turned seventeen,
and he delighted in concocting drivel of that sort, since his
chief purpose in life as a freshman wiseass was to question
everything he read and to make fun of it in any way he
could, but then his father dropped dead three months later,
and after Baumgartner returned from Newark, he stopped
throwing darts at Aristotle and moved on to other things.

Nevertheless, he has carried around those strange images in his head for years, millions upon millions of body-
souls driving their cars down massive, interconnecting roads
and highways, each person behind the wheel a human-sized
monad locked within the metal carapace of an insect-like
car, every man and woman from the multitudinous horde
alone in the midst of streaming, often perilous traffic, and
the body behind the wheel, which is also a mind, or a soul, or
an intelligence, is responsible for making hundreds of small
and large decisions to pilot the car safely to its destination.
Avoid wrong turns, steer clear of potholes and fallen objects
cluttering the road, and never, under any circumstances, take
an impulsive risk that could lead to a collision with another
car. Crashes can be fatal, after all, and once you are dead,
you remain dead for the rest of time.

That was how the book started to be born, Baumgartner
believes, from a corrosive vision of human life as a free-for-all

of careening, out-of-control cars speeding down highways of loneliness and potential death, but it wasn't until he started thinking about the word *automobile* that his ideas began to crystallize into what would become *Mysteries of the Wheel*. Automobile: a hybrid compound from ancient Greek (*autos*), Latin (*mobilis*), and nineteenth-century French (*mobile*) that means *self-moving* and is the formal term for what is generally referred to as a *car*. At the same time, it is also possible to think of human beings as self-moving creatures, and by taking those two unconnected thoughts and collapsing them into one far-fetched, flagrantly absurd notion, Baumgartner had found the metaphorical engine to drive his book forward. The car as person, the person as car, each one interchangeable with the other through a zigzagging, pseudo-philosophical discourse in the spirit of Swift, Kierkegaard, and other intellectual pranksters who have turned the world upside down in order to make their readers stand on their heads and try to reimagine a world that is right-side up. Funnyman Baumgartner. Sadly, these are not the happiest times for satire, and it remains to be seen if anyone will get the joke.

The book is divided into four sections, each one between sixty and seventy pages long: Introduction to Auto Mechanics, Breakdown in Motor City, Demolition Derby, and The Myth of the Self-Driving Car. Each one is simultaneously about individual and collective human life and the role cars play in that life, and while every chapter begins with a dry, mock-serious essay about the subject at hand, what follows after the introduction are stories, fifteen or twenty short narratives that range from invented fictions to reports of real events to fables, parables, and philosophical puzzles. Introduction to Auto Mechanics, for example, refers both to the human self (auto) and to learning how to drive and respect the rules of the road, as Baumgartner somehow manages to conflate the struggle to become a morally sound person and the effort to become a good driver. Breakdown in Motor City refers to the human body in various states of crisis (illnesses, fractured bones, epidemics) as well as to the mechanical difficulties that all cars run into at one time or another (flat tires, defective spark plugs, faulty carburetors). Demolition Derby charts what happens to a society when drivers give up following the rules of the road and assert their *God-given constitutional right* to personal freedom by running stop signs and red lights and mowing down any pedestrians who happen to be in the way. Not one word about the MAGA millions or the menace lurking in the White House, but Baumgartner's intentions are clear enough, and no further commentary is needed. Other examples follow of imaginary places that bear resemblances to Belfast, Sarajevo, and Rwanda but are never named as such. Last of all, The Myth of the Self-Driving Car addresses a future in which large segments of the population voluntarily relinquish their autonomy as free-thinking individuals and put their faith in a higher power (numbers), a disembodied Pythagorean force that necessarily escapes human understanding and is comprehensible only to the number-driven machines that have gradually taken control of the auto industry. Baumgartner ends his book with a story about a spectacular crash in Texas as four self-driving cars occupied by their sleeping owners converge at an intersection while traveling at eighty-six miles an hour and explode, bursting into flames and killing each one of the four men, who had all forgotten to program their cars before setting out on their appointments with death. In the final sentences, Baumgartner notes that the soon-to-be-published official police report will identify the cause of the catastrophe as *human error*.

He sends off the manuscript to Maddy Lifton on November twenty-fifth, the Monday before Thanksgiving. Describing his book as *bullshit on toast*, he warns her that Morris Heller and his son Miles will probably reject it as unpublishable, but incredibly enough they don't reject it, and by mid-December the decks have been cleared and Baumgartner can at last fix his thoughts entirely on Bebe Coen.

An absolute stranger to him just two months ago, she has now become the most important person in his life. They still haven't met and have seen each other only in photographs and on digital screens, but the truth is that Baumgartner already loves Beatrix Coen as much as the daughter he and Anna would have made together if such a thing had been possible. Tom Nozwitszki had not been wrong. In numerous small but indelible ways, Bebe resembles Anna. Not feature by feature, perhaps, but in spirit, in overall body

type, in the energy she emits in the presence of others. Bebe
is the one who has embraced Anna's work more thoroughly
than anyone else. For that reason alone, she deserves a place
of honor in Baumgartner's Hall of Beloveds, but having cor-
responded with her almost daily since mid-October, having
talked to her on telephones and zoom chats, he has witnessed
her mind at work and also knows how brilliant she is, and
yet, even more than that, he just plain likes her and can't
wait for her to show up on January fifth, twenty-one days
from now. Three interminable weeks, three short weeks, he
can no longer tell, but before long there will be no weeks,
and Baumgartner is half out of his skin with anticipation,
like a restless little boy counting down the days until school
lets out for the summer.

There is a problem, however. Bebe is planning to drive
from Ann Arbor to Princeton, and for fifty-seven different reasons, Baumgartner is alarmed. Michigan, Ohio, and
Pennsylvania can be miserable places in early January, and
with six hundred and fifteen miles to cover on a trip that
will demand roughly nine and a half hours of road time,
there is a strong chance that Lake Erie will dump one of
its snowstorms or ice storms or freezing rainstorms on her
small ten-year-old Toyota Camry and turn those six hundred
miles into one long danger zone. Then there is her insistence
on going solo, with no friend or companion to spell her behind the wheel or to help her in the event of an emergency.
Baumgartner suggests that she rethink her plan and travel by

train instead, but Bebe contends she will need her car once she arrives in New Jersey. Not so, Baumgartner replies, since he will be happy to lend her his car whenever she asks for it, but Bebe counters by saying she wouldn't think of inconveniencing him in that way, to which Baumgartner responds: Nonsense! If you don't want to borrow my car, I'll rent you one of your own for the visit. How's that? Out of the question, she answers. He's already spent too much money on her as it is, and she couldn't possibly accept anything more from him. Baumgartner immediately shoots back: Forget about the money. I can afford it! Twelve seconds later, by return text: I can't forget it!

They are locked in what his father used to call a *Mexican standoff.* The sweet and amiable Beatrix Coen turns out to be someone who cannot be pushed around, and woe to the person who dares to question her authority over herself or presumes to thwart her will. From time to time over the years, he had run into the same sorts of conflicts with Anna, who would blindside him with some festering complaint that had eluded his attention and go on the attack, angrily butting heads with him until at last he gave in and conceded the point. It didn't matter if she was right or wrong, since she was always right even when she was wrong, and Baumgartner soon learned that capitulation was the only reasonable defense, for once he had surrendered, the dispute was over and done with, wiped from memory within a matter of seconds. Is that the course he should follow with Bebe Coen—simply give in and let her have her way? Yes, the weather could be bad on January fourth and fifth, with wretched driving conditions all the way through, but there is an equal chance that she will sail eastward under balmy skies from the moment she starts out to the moment she pulls into his driveway the next evening. Impossible to know, impossible to know anything, but most of all he doesn't want to hammer away at her too hard and risk spoiling the visit, which would break his heart, Baumgartner realizes, since nothing means more to him now than the days or weeks or months they will be spending together in his house, where he has been living for more years than she has been alive. Therefore, just in advance of Christmas, Baumgartner backs down, tells her to do what she wants, and wishes her luck on the journey. The astute Ms. Coen, who understands that Baumgartner has already adopted her as his imaginary daughter and looks upon her as the second coming of his dead wife, is almost apologetic in her response to this change of heart, but as it had been with Anna in the old days, so it is with the young woman from Michigan now. The slate has been wiped clean, and their friendship is back on track.

Still, Baumgartner goes on worrying in silence. There is more to it than just the weather, after all, since accidents are just as likely to occur on dry roads as on wet or icy ones, and with more than six hundred miles of road to be covered, any one of ten thousand things can happen to her at any moment along the way. Christmas comes and goes, and by the twenty-seventh or twenty-eighth, Baumgartner has worked himself into a state of such anxiety that he is now in danger of falling into an out-and-out panic. He has little doubt that *Mysteries of the Wheel* is at least partly responsible for the agitation mounting within him, but what else could he have expected after two years of obsessive immersion in all things connected to cars, cars in and of themselves but also cars as representations of the human self as well as cars traveling along vast, interlocking networks of interstate highways with millions of other cars driven by millions of solitary people rushing headlong through the night—American society in a nutshell, the Land of the Free run amok along white-lined strips of ink-dark asphalt as ever-growing numbers of crazed, angry people abandon the rules of the road to participate in perpetual rounds of Demolition Derby, the number one smash-'em-up sport of the New Age. That was the central metaphor of Baumgartner's book, but now that Bebe Coen is about to traverse one-fifth of the American continent in a real car on a series of real roads between Michigan and New Jersey, the old man who will be awaiting her arrival on January fifth has been sucker-punched by his own imagination and finds himself powerless not to amplify and even distort the gravity of the dangers that lie in front of her. Not that he is necessarily wrong to be conjuring up the worst possible outcomes, but fatal accidents are statistically rare when one considers the total number of miles driven by the many millions of cars on the road, and if Baumgartner

PAUL AUSTER

were thinking more clearly, he would understand that his panic has transformed the long-shot odds of Bebe's death on Route 80 in central Pennsylvania into a sure thing. But he is not thinking clearly, and therefore his waking hours are now lived in a sweatbox of continual dread.

The book first of all, perhaps, but not most of all, since Baumgartner knows that Anna's death is mixed up in this as well, the final day on the Cape Cod beach when she ran off into the water before he had a chance to stop her. Anna was already on her feet when she announced she was going in for *a last dip*, and Baumgartner was sprawled out on a towel reading a book, but in spite of telling her that it was getting late and they should be going back to the house, she laughed him off and was already running by the time he managed to stand up, so far in front of him by then that there was no earthly way for him to have caught up with her. Not enough time. But with Bebe there has been plenty of time, more than a month for him to have talked her into leaving her car in Michigan and taking the train instead, but for all his efforts he has gotten nowhere with her, and now it is too late, and if anything should happen to her on the road between there and here, Baumgartner feels that it will kill him. He has never thought such a thought at any point in his life until now, but unless Bebe Coen makes it to his house safe and unharmed, he feels in his bones that he will die.

They have a long talk by telephone on the third. Baumgartner does everything he can to suppress his fears

196

and keep his voice under control, for Bebe is in excellent spirits this afternoon, all packed and ready to hit the road in the morning, and the last thing Baumgartner wants is to contaminate her happiness with his dreary forebodings. Instead, he talks to her about the promising weather forecast for tomorrow (mid-thirties, partly cloudy, ten percent chance of precipitation) and asks her when she thinks she will make it to Pittsburgh, the midway point of the journey, where she is planning to spend the night at the house of old friends of her parents, a pair of married research scientists who work at Carnegie Mellon. Difficult to know for sure, Bebe says, since she's going out for dinner with a group of friends tonight in Ann Arbor, and it all depends on how long the gathering lasts and when she goes to bed, which in turn will decide how late or early she gets up in the morning and therefore how late or early she will be climbing into her car to set off for Pittsburgh. They are engaged in one of the most banal conversations imaginable, but the more Baumgartner listens to Bebe talk, the less anxious he feels about tomorrow and the day after, no doubt because even the most ordinary words that come from her mouth are imbued with some mesmerizing, transcendent quality that makes them sound as important as a Shakespeare sonnet or the preamble to the Declaration of the Rights of Man. Anna had that quality as well, not just in her voice but in her power to transform the most ordinary movements of the body into acts of sublime self-expression and grace, the eloquence of her fingers as she turned the pages of a book, for example, or the stately rotations of her wrists as she folded a napkin or a towel—the simplest, most commonplace human gestures glowing like miracles in the forge of ignited selfhood. Anna Blume and Beatrix Coen, the two bookends of his life, Baumgartner says to himself, and as he wishes Bebe a smooth and uneventful trip tomorrow, he holds back from saying the one thing he so desperately wants to say next: *Drive carefully, I beg of you.* It takes a supreme effort for him not to say those words, but even so it is as if Bebe can hear them anyway, for no sooner does he not say them than she begins to laugh and says: Don't worry, Sy, I promise to drive carefully.

It is half past one on January 3, 2020. Baumgartner has just hung up the phone, and the question to be answered now is what he should do with himself for the rest of the day, not to speak of tomorrow and the day after tomorrow as well. He does not expect to hear from her again until after she makes it to her parents' friends in Pittsburgh—assuming nothing happens to her on the first leg of the trip—but if all goes as hoped for, it will be a good twenty-six to twenty-eight hours from now before she gets there, and who knows if she will remember to contact him when she does? Baumgartner has made no plans, and he is feeling too on edge to start going through Anna's papers again or to work on anything else. A walk might do him some good, he thinks, but it's bloody freezing today, and if he wants to get out of the house and move around a bit, the only comfortable solution is to do it by car. So be it, he says to himself, he'll drive over to the liquor store and stock up on some more booze and an extra case of wine, and if he can't think of anything else to do after that, he'll call around and see if one of his friends is available tonight for an impromptu restaurant dinner.

So Baumgartner bundles up in his warmest winter clothes and warmest winter jacket, goes off to the garage, and plants his body behind the wheel of his four-year-old Subaru Crosstrek, a hybrid model that alternately runs on gasoline and battery-generated electric power. When Baumgartner starts up the engine and drives away from the house, he realizes that he has no interest in going into town or adding to his stock of wines and spirits or chancing an unwelcome encounter with someone he knows but doesn't care about that will force him into exchanging vapid pleasantries for two or three endless minutes, so rather than head toward the familiar world of the shopping district, Baumgartner turns in the opposite direction, and before long he is driving south, away from the crowded commercial highways and blinking lights toward open country, a sparse nowhere with fewer and fewer houses and smaller and smaller roads. He believes he is approaching the area called the Pine Barrens, but he isn't quite sure, given how many years it has been since he and Anna set off one Sunday afternoon to explore this mysteriously empty territory and he no longer remembers the details, except that they stopped somewhere to eat a picnic lunch and that as they spread their blanket on the sandy soil and he looked over at Anna's beautiful, shining face, he was flooded with a feeling of happiness so powerful that tears began to gather in his eyes and he said to himself: Remember this moment, little man, remember it for the rest of your life, for nothing more important will ever happen to you than what is happening to you right now.

He remembers remembering the feeling and carrying it around with him for years afterward, but the particulars of the place where he felt those things have mostly vanished from his mind, so much so that he can't be sure if he has returned to that spot or is in fact somewhere else. How long has it been since he climbed into his car and left the house? Forty or forty-five minutes, he would think, not much longer than that, but already the light has begun to change, since these are the weeks just after the winter solstice and the days are still short, ever so short, and as he turns right onto a narrow strip of road that cuts through a dense profusion of pines, he sees something out of the corner of his left eye, and lo and behold it is a deer, bounding forth from the woods on the left side of the road, and just like that, without a moment's hesitation, Baumgartner instinctively swerves to the left and avoids crashing into the deer, which has already crossed the road and disappeared into the woods on the other side. Baumgartner stops the car for a moment to regroup after such a close call, marveling at how quick his reflexes still are at seventy-two but nevertheless rattled by the suddenness of the event, which couldn't have lasted more than three or four seconds from start to finish. Eventually, he starts up the car again and drives on, at one point going past a house and a few hundred yards after that another house, but much as he feels that the time has come to begin heading home, he has yet to come upon a crossroad that would allow him to turn left or right and start angling his way to the north. He therefore drives on, searching for a small opening in the trees along the side of the road in order to turn around and go back along the same road he has already covered from the opposite direction, but before he can detect any breach in the pines, another deer is bounding out of the woods, this time from the right side of the road, and if Baumgartner swerves to the left, he will collide with the deer, so he swerves to the right, misses the deer, careens off the edge of the road, and crashes into a tree. He has been driving slowly, no more than twenty-eight or thirty miles an hour, but the impact is nevertheless both abrupt and violent, and even though Baumgartner is wearing his seat belt, he pitches forward and bangs his forehead into the steering wheel hard enough to pierce the skin and for a trickle of blood to be descending toward his right eye. For some reason, the airbag didn't inflate. A malfunction, perhaps, or else the impact of the car crashing into the tree wasn't strong enough to trigger the mechanism.

Baumgartner is conscious and not in pain. Nevertheless, he feels stunned by what has just happened, and as he wipes away the blood with his handkerchief, he marvels that a gash that has produced so much blood should hurt so little—in fact, not hurt at all. For the next few minutes, he remains in the driver's seat and doesn't move, thinking about what he should do next. Examine the car first, he decides, and if there is no serious damage and the Subaru is still functioning, he will climb back into the car, turn around, and drive back to Princeton. He steps out into the cold, cold air and discovers that the grille has been badly dented. Not enough to cause any mechanical difficulties, he thinks, but when he gets back into the car and pushes the ignition button, nothing happens. Silence from the battery, silence from the engine, a true and perhaps permanent breakdown in the heart of motor city, and since Baumgartner knows nothing about auto mechanics and would not be capable of fixing the problem himself, he concludes there is nothing to be done but to turn up the collar of his jacket, thrust his hands into his pockets, and begin walking through the dim winter light toward the houses he passed earlier. And so, with the wind in his face and blood still trickling from the wound in his forehead, our hero goes off in search of help, and when he comes to the first house and knocks on the door, the final chapter in the saga of S.T. Baumgartner begins.